Presented to Purchase College
by
Gary Waller, PhD Cambridge

State University of New York
Distinguished Professor

Professor
of Literature & Cultural
Studies, and Theatre &
Performance, 1995-2019
Provost 1995-2004

JOHN WEBSTER

THE WHITE DEVIL

THE WHITE DEVIL

BY

JOHN WEBSTER

THE WHITE DEVIL

By

JOHN WEBSTER

TO THE READER

In publishing this tragedy, I do but challenge myself that liberty, which other men have taken before me; not that I affect praise by it, for, nos hæc novimus esse nihil, only since it was acted in so dull a time of winter, presented in so open and black a theatre, that it wanted (that which is the only grace and setting-out of a tragedy) a full and understanding auditory; and that since that time I have noted, most of the people that come to that playhouse resemble those ignorant asses (who, visiting stationers' shops, their use is not to inquire for good books, but new books), I present it to the general view with this confidence:

Nec rhoncos metues maligniorum,
Nec scombris tunicas dabis molestas.

If it be objected this is no true dramatic poem, I shall easily confess it, non potes in nugas dicere plura meas, ipse ego quam dixi; willingly, and not ignorantly, in this kind have I faulted: For should a man present to such an auditory, the most sententious tragedy that ever was written, observing all the critical laws as height of style, and gravity of person, enrich it with the sententious Chorus, and, as it were Life and Death, in the passionate and weighty Nuntius: yet after all this divine rapture, O dura messorum ilia, the breath that comes from the incapable multitude is able to poison it; and, ere it be acted, let the author resolve to fix to every scene this of Horace:

—Hæc hodie porcis comedenda relinques.

To those who report I was a long time in finishing this tragedy, I confess I do not write with a goose-quill winged with two feathers; and if they will need make it my fault, I must answer them with that of Euripides to Alcestides, a tragic writer: Alcestides objecting that Euripides had only, in three days composed three verses, whereas himself had written three hundred: Thou tallest truth (quoth he), but here 's the difference, thine shall only be read for three days, whereas mine shall continue for three ages.

Detraction is the sworn friend to ignorance: for mine own part, I have ever truly cherished my good opinion of other men's worthy labours, especially of that full and heightened style of Mr. Chapman, the laboured and understanding works of Mr. Johnson, the no less worthy composures of the both worthily excellent Mr. Beaumont and Mr. Fletcher; and lastly (without wrong last to be named), the right happy and copious industry of Mr. Shakespeare, Mr. Dekker, and Mr. Heywood, wishing what I write may be read by their light: protesting that, in the strength of mine own judgment, I know them so worthy, that though I rest silent in my own work, yet to most of theirs I dare (without flattery) fix that of Martial:

—non norunt hæc monumenta mori.

DRAMATIS PERSONÆ

MONTICELSO, a Cardinal; afterwards Pope PAUL the Fourth.
FRANCISCO DE MEDICIS, Duke of Florence; in the 5th Act disguised for a
  Moor, under the name of MULINASSAR.
BRACHIANO, otherwise PAULO GIORDANO URSINI, Duke of Brachiano, Husband
  to ISABELLA, and in love with VITTORIA.
GIOVANNI—his Son by ISABELLA.
LODOVICO, an Italian Count, but decayed.
ANTONELLI, | his Friends, and Dependants of the Duke of Florence.
GASPARO, |
CAMILLO, Husband to VITTORIA.
HORTENSIO, one of BRACHIANO's Officers.
MARCELLO, an Attendant of the Duke of Florence, and Brother to VITTORIA.
FLAMINEO, his Brother; Secretary to BRACHIANO.
JACQUES, a Moor, Servant to GIOVANNI.
ISABELLA, Sister to FRANCISCO DE MEDICI, and Wife to BRACHIANO.
VITTORIA COROMBONA, a Venetian Lady; first married to CAMILLO, afterwards
  to BRACHIANO.
CORNELIA, Mother to VITTORIA, FLAMINEO, and MARCELLO.
ZANCHE, a Moor, Servant to VITTORIA.
Ambassadors, Courtiers, Lawyers, Officers, Physicians, Conjurer,
  Armourer, Attendants.

THE SCENE—ITALY

ACT I

SCENE I

Enter Count Lodovico, Antonelli, and Gasparo

Lodo. Banish'd!

Ant. It griev'd me much to hear the sentence.

Lodo. Ha, ha, O Democritus, thy gods
  That govern the whole world! courtly reward
  And punishment. Fortune 's a right whore:
  If she give aught, she deals it in small parcels,
  That she may take away all at one swoop.
  This 'tis to have great enemies! God 'quite them.
  Your wolf no longer seems to be a wolf
  Than when she 's hungry.

Gas. You term those enemies,
  Are men of princely rank.

Lodo. Oh, I pray for them:
  The violent thunder is adored by those
  Are pasht in pieces by it.

Ant. Come, my lord,
  You are justly doom'd; look but a little back
  Into your former life: you have in three years
  Ruin'd the noblest earldom.

Gas. Your followers
  Have swallowed you, like mummia, and being sick
  With such unnatural and horrid physic,
  Vomit you up i' th' kennel.

Ant. All the damnable degrees
  Of drinking have you stagger'd through. One citizen,
  Is lord of two fair manors, call'd you master,
  Only for caviare.

Gas. Those noblemen
  Which were invited to your prodigal feasts,
  (Wherein the phnix scarce could 'scape your throats)
  Laugh at your misery, as fore-deeming you
  An idle meteor, which drawn forth, the earth
  Would be soon lost i' the air.

Ant. Jest upon you,
  And say you were begotten in an earthquake,
  You have ruin'd such fair lordships.

Lodo. Very good.
  This well goes with two buckets: I must tend
  The pouring out of either.

Gas. Worse than these.
  You have acted certain murders here in Rome,
  Bloody and full of horror.

Lodo. 'Las, they were flea-bitings:
  Why took they not my head then?

Gas. O, my lord!
  The law doth sometimes mediate, thinks it good
  Not ever to steep violent sins in blood:
  This gentle penance may both end your crimes,
  And in the example better these bad times.

Lodo. So; but I wonder then some great men 'scape
  This banishment: there 's Paulo Giordano Ursini,
  The Duke of Brachiano, now lives in Rome,
  And by close panderism seeks to prostitute
  The honour of Vittoria Corombona:
  Vittoria, she that might have got my pardon
  For one kiss to the duke.

Ant. Have a full man within you:
  We see that trees bear no such pleasant fruit
  There where they grew first, as where they are new set.
  Perfumes, the more they are chaf'd, the more they render
  Their pleasing scents, and so affliction
  Expresseth virtue fully, whether true,
  Or else adulterate.

Lodo. Leave your painted comforts;
  I 'll make Italian cut-works in their guts
  If ever I return.

Gas. Oh, sir.

Lodo. I am patient.
  I have seen some ready to be executed,
  Give pleasant looks, and money, and grown familiar
  With the knave hangman; so do I; I thank them,
  And would account them nobly merciful,
  Would they dispatch me quickly.

Ant. Fare you well;
  We shall find time, I doubt not, to repeal
  Your banishment.

Lodo. I am ever bound to you.
  This is the world's alms; pray make use of it.
  Great men sell sheep, thus to be cut in pieces,
  When first they have shorn them bare, and sold their fleeces.
                    [Exeunt

3

SCENE II

Enter Brachiano, Camillo, Flamineo, Vittoria

Brach. Your best of rest.

Vit. Unto my lord the duke,
  The best of welcome. More lights: attend the duke.
                      [Exeunt Camillo and Vittoria.

Brach. Flamineo.

Flam. My lord.

Brach. Quite lost, Flamineo.

Flam. Pursue your noble wishes, I am prompt
  As lightning to your service. O my lord!
  The fair Vittoria, my happy sister,
  Shall give you present audience—Gentlemen, [Whisper.
  Let the caroch go on—and 'tis his pleasure
  You put out all your torches and depart.

Brach. Are we so happy?

Flam. Can it be otherwise?
  Observ'd you not to-night, my honour'd lord,
  Which way soe'er you went, she threw her eyes?
  I have dealt already with her chambermaid,
  Zanche the Moor, and she is wondrous proud
  To be the agent for so high a spirit.

Brach. We are happy above thought, because 'bove merit.

Flam. 'Bove merit! we may now talk freely: 'bove merit! what is 't you doubt? her coyness! that 's but the superficies of lust most women have; yet why should ladies blush to hear that named, which they do not fear to handle? Oh, they are politic; they know our desire is increased by the difficulty of enjoying; whereas satiety is a blunt, weary, and drowsy passion. If the buttery-hatch at court stood continually open, there would be nothing so passionate crowding, nor hot suit after the beverage.

Brach. Oh, but her jealous husband——

Flam. Hang him; a gilder that hath his brains perished with quicksilver is not more cold in the liver. The great barriers moulted not more feathers, than he hath shed hairs, by the confession of his doctor. An

4

Irish gamester that will play himself naked, and then wage all
downward, at hazard, is not more venturous. So unable to please a
woman, that, like a Dutch doublet, all his back is shrunk into his
breeches.
Shroud you within this closet, good my lord;
Some trick now must be thought on to divide
My brother-in-law from his fair bed-fellow.

Brach. Oh, should she fail to come——

Flam. I must not have your lordship thus unwisely amorous. I myself have not loved a lady,
and pursued her with a great deal of under-age protestation, whom some three or four
gallants that have enjoyed would with all their hearts have been glad to have been rid of.
'Tis just like a summer bird-cage in a garden: the birds that are without despair to get in,
and the birds that are within despair and are in a consumption for fear they shall never get
out. Away, away, my lord. [Exit Brachiano as Camillo enters.

See here he comes. This fellow by his apparel
Some men would judge a politician;
But call his wit in question, you shall find it
Merely an ass in 's foot-cloth. How now, brother?
What, travelling to bed with your kind wife?

Cam. I assure you, brother, no. My voyage lies
More northerly, in a far colder clime.
I do not well remember, I protest,
When I last lay with her.

Flam. Strange you should lose your count.

Cam. We never lay together, but ere morning
There grew a flaw between us.

Flam. 'T had been your part
To have made up that flaw.

Cam. True, but she loathes I should be seen in 't.

Flam. Why, sir, what 's the matter?

Cam. The duke your master visits me, I thank him;
And I perceive how, like an earnest bowler,
He very passionately leans that way
he should have his bowl run.

Flam. I hope you do not think——

5

Cam. That nobleman bowl booty? faith, his cheek
  Hath a most excellent bias: it would fain
  Jump with my mistress.

Flam. Will you be an ass,
  Despite your Aristotle? or a cuckold,
  Contrary to your Ephemerides,
  Which shows you under what a smiling planet
  You were first swaddled?

Cam. Pew wew, sir; tell me not
  Of planets nor of Ephemerides.
  A man may be made cuckold in the day-time,
  When the stars' eyes are out.

Flam. Sir, good-bye you;
  I do commit you to your pitiful pillow
  Stuffed with horn-shavings.

Cam. Brother!

Flam. God refuse me.
  Might I advise you now, your only course
  Were to lock up your wife.

Cam. 'Twere very good.

Flam. Bar her the sight of revels.

Cam. Excellent.

Flam. Let her not go to church, but, like a hound
  In leon, at your heels.

Cam. 'Twere for her honour.

Flam. And so you should be certain in one fortnight,
  Despite her chastity or innocence,
  To be cuckolded, which yet is in suspense:
  This is my counsel, and I ask no fee for 't.

Cam. Come, you know not where my nightcap wrings me.

Flam. Wear it a' th' old fashion; let your large ears come through, it will be more easy—nay,
I will be bitter—bar your wife of her entertainment: women are more willingly and more
gloriously chaste, when they are least restrained of their liberty. It seems you would be a

fine capricious, mathematically jealous coxcomb; take the height of your own horns with a Jacob's staff, afore they are up. These politic enclosures for paltry mutton, makes more rebellion in the flesh, than all the provocative electuaries doctors have uttered since last jubilee.

Cam. This doth not physic me——

Flam. It seems you are jealous: I 'll show you the error of it by a familiar example: I have seen a pair of spectacles fashioned with such perspective art, that lay down but one twelve pence a' th' board, 'twill appear as if there were twenty; now should you wear a pair of these spectacles, and see your wife tying her shoe, you would imagine twenty hands were taking up of your wife's clothes, and this would put you into a horrible causeless fury.

Cam. The fault there, sir, is not in the eyesight.

Flam. True, but they that have the yellow jaundice think all objects they look on to be yellow. Jealousy is worse; her fits present to a man, like so many bubbles in a basin of water, twenty several crabbed faces, many times makes his own shadow his cuckold-maker. [Enter Vittoria Corombona.] See, she comes; what reason have you to be jealous of this creature? what an ignorant ass or flattering knave might be counted, that should write sonnets to her eyes, or call her brow the snow of Ida, or ivory of Corinth; or compare her hair to the blackbird's bill, when 'tis liker the blackbird's feather? This is all. Be wise; I will make you friends, and you shall go to bed together. Marry, look you, it shall not be your seeking. Do you stand upon that, by any means: walk you aloof; I would not have you seen in 't.—Sister [my lord attend you in the banqueting-house,] your husband is wondrous discontented.

Vit. I did nothing to displease him; I carved to him at supper-time.

Flam. [You need not have carved him, in faith; they say he is a capon already. I must now seemingly fall out with you.] Shall a gentleman so well descended as Camillo [a lousy slave, that within this twenty years rode with the black guard in the duke's carriage, 'mongst spits and dripping-pans!]—

Cam. Now he begins to tickle her.

Flam. An excellent scholar [one that hath a head fill'd with calves' brains without any sage in them,] come crouching in the hams to you for a night's lodging? [that hath an itch in 's hams, which like the fire at the glass-house hath not gone out this seven years] Is he not a courtly gentleman? [when he wears white satin, one would take him by his black muzzle to be no other creature than a maggot] You are a goodly foil, I confess, well set out [but cover'd with a false stone— yon counterfeit diamond].

Cam. He will make her know what is in me.

Flam. Come, my lord attends you; thou shalt go to bed to my lord.

Cam. Now he comes to 't.

Flam. [With a relish as curious as a vintner going to taste new wine.]
  [To Camillo.] I am opening your case hard.

Cam. A virtuous brother, o' my credit!

Flam. He will give thee a ring with a philosopher's stone in it.

Cam. Indeed, I am studying alchemy.

Flam. Thou shalt lie in a bed stuffed with turtle's feathers; swoon in perfumed linen, like the fellow was smothered in roses. So perfect shall be thy happiness, that as men at sea think land, and trees, and ships, go that way they go; so both heaven and earth shall seem to go your voyage. Shalt meet him; 'tis fix'd, with nails of diamonds to inevitable necessity.

Vit. How shalt rid him hence?

Flam. [I will put brize in 's tail, set him gadding presently.] I have almost wrought her to it; I find her coming: but, might I advise you now, for this night I would not lie with her, I would cross her humour to make her more humble.

Cam. Shall I, shall I?

Flam. It will show in you a supremacy of judgment.

Cam. True, and a mind differing from the tumultuary opinion; for, quæ
  negata, grata.

Flam. Right: you are the adamant shall draw her to you, though you keep
  distance off.

Cam. A philosophical reason.

Flam. Walk by her a' th' nobleman's fashion, and tell her you will lie with her at the end of the progress.

Cam. Vittoria, I cannot be induc'd, or as a man would say, incited——

Vit. To do what, sir?

Cam. To lie with you to-night. Your silkworm used to fast every third day, and the next following spins the better. To-morrow at night, I am for you.

Vit. You 'll spin a fair thread, trust to 't.

Flam. But do you hear, I shall have you steal to her chamber about midnight.

Cam. Do you think so? why look you, brother, because you shall not say I 'll gull you, take the key, lock me into the chamber, and say you shall be sure of me.

Flam. In troth I will; I 'll be your jailor once.

Cam. A pox on 't, as I am a Christian! tell me to-morrow how scurvily she takes my unkind parting.

Flam. I will.

Cam. Didst thou not mark the jest of the silkworm?
  Good-night; in faith, I will use this trick often.

Flam. Do, do, do. [Exit Camillo. So, now you are safe. Ha, ha, ha, thou entanglest thyself in thine own work like a silkworm. [Enter Brachiano.] Come, sister, darkness hides your blush. Women are like cursed dogs: civility keeps them tied all daytime, but they are let loose at midnight; then they do most good, or most mischief. My lord, my lord!

Zanche brings out a carpet, spreads it, and lays on it two fair cushions.
  Enter Cornelia listening, but unperceived.

Brach. Give credit: I could wish time would stand still,
  And never end this interview, this hour;
  But all delight doth itself soon'st devour.
  Let me into your bosom, happy lady,
  Pour out, instead of eloquence, my vows.
  Loose me not, madam, for if you forgo me,
  I am lost eternally.

Vit. Sir, in the way of pity,
  I wish you heart-whole.

Brach. You are a sweet physician.

Vit. Sure, sir, a loathed cruelty in ladies
  Is as to doctors many funerals:
  It takes away their credit.

Brach. Excellent creature!
  We call the cruel fair; what name for you
  That are so merciful?

Zan. See now they close.

Flam. Most happy union.

Corn. [Aside.] My fears are fall'n upon me: oh, my heart!
 My son the pander! now I find our house
 Sinking to ruin. Earthquakes leave behind,
 Where they have tyranniz'd, iron, or lead, or stone;
 But woe to ruin, violent lust leaves none.

Brach. What value is this jewel?

Vit. 'Tis the ornament of a weak fortune.

Brach. In sooth, I 'll have it; nay, I will but change
 My jewel for your jewel.

Flam. Excellent;
 His jewel for her jewel: well put in, duke.

Brach. Nay, let me see you wear it.

Vit. Here, sir?

Brach. Nay, lower, you shall wear my jewel lower.

Flam. That 's better: she must wear his jewel lower.

Vit. To pass away the time, I 'll tell your grace
 A dream I had last night.

Brach. Most wishedly.

Vit. A foolish idle dream:
 Methought I walked about the mid of night
 Into a churchyard, where a goodly yew-tree
 Spread her large root in ground: under that yew,
 As I sat sadly leaning on a grave,
 Chequer'd with cross-sticks, there came stealing in
 Your duchess and my husband; one of them
 A pickaxe bore, th' other a rusty spade,
 And in rough terms they 'gan to challenge me
 About this yew.

Brach. That tree?

Vit. This harmless yew;
 They told me my intent was to root up
 That well-grown yew, and plant i' the stead of it
 A wither'd blackthorn; and for that they vow'd

To bury me alive. My husband straight
With pickaxe 'gan to dig, and your fell duchess
With shovel, like a fury, voided out
The earth and scatter'd bones: Lord, how methought
I trembled, and yet for all this terror
I could not pray.

Flam. No; the devil was in your dream.

Vit. When to my rescue there arose, methought,
A whirlwind, which let fall a massy arm
From that strong plant;
And both were struck dead by that sacred yew,
In that base shallow grave that was their due.

Flam. Excellent devil!
She hath taught him in a dream
To make away his duchess and her husband.

Brach. Sweetly shall I interpret this your dream.
You are lodg'd within his arms who shall protect you
From all the fevers of a jealous husband,
From the poor envy of our phlegmatic duchess.
I 'll seat you above law, and above scandal;
Give to your thoughts the invention of delight,
And the fruition; nor shall government
Divide me from you longer, than a care
To keep you great: you shall to me at once
Be dukedom, health, wife, children, friends, and all.

Corn. [Advancing.] Woe to light hearts, they still forerun our fall!

Flam. What fury raised thee up? away, away. [Exit Zanche.

Corn. What make you here, my lord, this dead of night?
Never dropp'd mildew on a flower here till now.

Flam. I pray, will you go to bed then,
Lest you be blasted?

Corn. O that this fair garden
Had with all poison'd herbs of Thessaly
At first been planted; made a nursery
For witchcraft, rather than a burial plot
For both your honours!

Vit. Dearest mother, hear me.

Corn. O, thou dost make my brow bend to the earth.
  Sooner than nature! See the curse of children!
  In life they keep us frequently in tears;
  And in the cold grave leave us in pale fears.

Brach. Come, come, I will not hear you.

Vit. Dear my lord.

Corn. Where is thy duchess now, adulterous duke?
  Thou little dream'st this night she 's come to Rome.

Flam. How! come to Rome!

Vit. The duchess!

Brach. She had been better——

Corn. The lives of princes should like dials move,
  Whose regular example is so strong,
  They make the times by them go right, or wrong.

Flam. So, have you done?

Corn. Unfortunate Camillo!

Vit. I do protest, if any chaste denial,
  If anything but blood could have allay'd
  His long suit to me——

Corn. I will join with thee,
  To the most woeful end e'er mother kneel'd:
  If thou dishonour thus thy husband's bed,
  Be thy life short as are the funeral tears
  In great men's——

Brach. Fie, fie, the woman's mad.

Corn. Be thy act Judas-like; betray in kissing:
  May'st thou be envied during his short breath,
  And pitied like a wretch after his death!

Vit. O me accurs'd! [Exit.

Flam. Are you out of your wits? my lord,
  I 'll fetch her back again.

Brach. No, I 'll to bed:
  Send Doctor Julio to me presently.
  Uncharitable woman! thy rash tongue
  Hath rais'd a fearful and prodigious storm:
  Be thou the cause of all ensuing harm. [Exit.

Flam. Now, you that stand so much upon your honour,
  Is this a fitting time a' night, think you,
  To send a duke home without e'er a man?
  I would fain know where lies the mass of wealth
  Which you have hoarded for my maintenance,
  That I may bear my beard out of the level
  Of my lord's stirrup.

Corn. What! because we are poor
  Shall we be vicious?

Flam. Pray, what means have you
  To keep me from the galleys, or the gallows?
  My father prov'd himself a gentleman,
  Sold all 's land, and, like a fortunate fellow,
  Died ere the money was spent. You brought me up
  At Padua, I confess, where I protest,
  For want of means—the University judge me—
  I have been fain to heel my tutor's stockings,
  At least seven years; conspiring with a beard,
  Made me a graduate; then to this duke's service,
  I visited the court, whence I return'd
  More courteous, more lecherous by far,
  But not a suit the richer. And shall I,
  Having a path so open, and so free
  To my preferment, still retain your milk
  In my pale forehead? No, this face of mine
  I 'll arm, and fortify with lusty wine,
  'Gainst shame and blushing.

Corn. O that I ne'er had borne thee!

Flam. So would I;
 I would the common'st courtesan in Rome
 Had been my mother, rather than thyself.
 Nature is very pitiful to whores,
 To give them but few children, yet those children
 Plurality of fathers; they are sure
 They shall not want. Go, go,
 Complain unto my great lord cardinal;
 It may be he will justify the act.
 Lycurgus wonder'd much, men would provide
 Good stallions for their mares, and yet would suffer
 Their fair wives to be barren.

Corn. Misery of miseries! [Exit.

Flam. The duchess come to court! I like not that.
 We are engag'd to mischief, and must on;
 As rivers to find out the ocean
 Flow with crook bendings beneath forced banks,
 Or as we see, to aspire some mountain's top,
 The way ascends not straight, but imitates
 The subtle foldings of a winter's snake,
 So who knows policy and her true aspect,
 Shall find her ways winding and indirect.

ACT II

SCENE I

Enter Francisco de Medicis, Cardinal Monticelso, Marcello, Isabella, young Giovanni, with little Jacques the Moor

Fran. Have you not seen your husband since you arrived?

Isab. Not yet, sir.

Fran. Surely he is wondrous kind;
  If I had such a dove-house as Camillo's,
  I would set fire on 't were 't but to destroy
  The polecats that haunt to it—My sweet cousin!

Giov. Lord uncle, you did promise me a horse,
  And armour.

Fran. That I did, my pretty cousin.
  Marcello, see it fitted.

Marc. My lord, the duke is here.

Fran. Sister, away; you must not yet be seen.

Isab. I do beseech you,
  Entreat him mildly, let not your rough tongue
  Set us at louder variance; all my wrongs
  Are freely pardon'd; and I do not doubt,
  As men to try the precious unicorn's horn
  Make of the powder a preservative circle,
  And in it put a spider, so these arms
  Shall charm his poison, force it to obeying,
  And keep him chaste from an infected straying.

Fran. I wish it may. Begone. [Exit Isabella as Brachiano and Flamineo
  enter.] Void the chamber.
  You are welcome; will you sit?—I pray, my lord,
  Be you my orator, my heart 's too full;
  I 'll second you anon.

Mont. Ere I begin,
  Let me entreat your grace forgo all passion,
  Which may be raised by my free discourse.

Brach. As silent as i' th' church: you may proceed.

Mont. It is a wonder to your noble friends,
  That you, having as 'twere enter'd the world
  With a free scepter in your able hand,
  And having to th' use of nature well applied
  High gifts of learning, should in your prime age
  Neglect your awful throne for the soft down
  Of an insatiate bed. O my lord,
  The drunkard after all his lavish cups
  Is dry, and then is sober; so at length,
  When you awake from this lascivious dream,
  Repentance then will follow, like the sting
  Plac'd in the adder's tail. Wretched are princes
  When fortune blasteth but a petty flower
  Of their unwieldy crowns, or ravisheth
  But one pearl from their scepter; but alas!
  When they to wilful shipwreck lose good fame,
  All princely titles perish with their name.

Brach. You have said, my lord——

Mont. Enough to give you taste
  How far I am from flattering your greatness.

Brach. Now you that are his second, what say you?
  Do not like young hawks fetch a course about;
  Your game flies fair, and for you.

Fran. Do not fear it:
  I 'll answer you in your own hawking phrase.
  Some eagles that should gaze upon the sun
  Seldom soar high, but take their lustful ease,
  Since they from dunghill birds their prey can seize.
  You know Vittoria?

Brach. Yes.

Fran. You shift your shirt there,
  When you retire from tennis?

Brach. Happily.

Fran. Her husband is lord of a poor fortune,
  Yet she wears cloth of tissue.

Brach. What of this?
  Will you urge that, my good lord cardinal,
  As part of her confession at next shrift,
  And know from whence it sails?

Fran. She is your strumpet——

Brach. Uncivil sir, there 's hemlock in thy breath,
  And that black slander. Were she a whore of mine,
  All thy loud cannons, and thy borrow'd Switzers,
  Thy galleys, nor thy sworn confederates,
  Durst not supplant her.

Fran. Let 's not talk on thunder.
  Thou hast a wife, our sister; would I had given
  Both her white hands to death, bound and lock'd fast
  In her last winding sheet, when I gave thee
  But one.

Brach. Thou hadst given a soul to God then.

Fran. True:
  Thy ghostly father, with all his absolution,
  Shall ne'er do so by thee.

Brach. Spit thy poison.

Fran. I shall not need; lust carries her sharp whip
  At her own girdle. Look to 't, for our anger
  Is making thunderbolts.

Brach. Thunder! in faith,
  They are but crackers.

Fran. We 'll end this with the cannon.

Brach. Thou 'lt get naught by it, but iron in thy wounds,
  And gunpowder in thy nostrils.

Fran. Better that,
  Than change perfumes for plasters.

Brach. Pity on thee!
  'Twere good you 'd show your slaves or men condemn'd,
  Your new-plough'd forehead. Defiance! and I 'll meet thee,
  Even in a thicket of thy ablest men.

Mont. My lords, you shall not word it any further
  Without a milder limit.

Fran. Willingly.

Brach. Have you proclaim'd a triumph, that you bait
  A lion thus?

Mont. My lord!

Brach. I am tame, I am tame, sir.

Fran. We send unto the duke for conference
  'Bout levies 'gainst the pirates; my lord duke
  Is not at home: we come ourself in person;
  Still my lord duke is busied. But we fear
  When Tiber to each prowling passenger
  Discovers flocks of wild ducks, then, my lord—
  'Bout moulting time I mean—we shall be certain
  To find you sure enough, and speak with you.

Brach. Ha!

Fran. A mere tale of a tub: my words are idle.
  But to express the sonnet by natural reason,
                            [Enter Giovanni.
  When stags grow melancholic you 'll find the season.

Mont. No more, my lord; here comes a champion
  Shall end the difference between you both;
  Your son, the Prince Giovanni. See, my lords,
  What hopes you store in him; this is a casket
  For both your crowns, and should be held like dear.
  Now is he apt for knowledge; therefore know
  It is a more direct and even way,
  To train to virtue those of princely blood,
  By examples than by precepts: if by examples,
  Whom should he rather strive to imitate
  Than his own father? be his pattern then,
  Leave him a stock of virtue that may last,
  Should fortune rend his sails, and split his mast.

Brach. Your hand, boy: growing to a soldier?

Giov. Give me a pike.

Fran. What, practising your pike so young, fair cousin?

Giov. Suppose me one of Homer's frogs, my lord,
  Tossing my bulrush thus. Pray, sir, tell me,
  Might not a child of good discretion
  Be leader to an army?

Fran. Yes, cousin, a young prince
  Of good discretion might.

Giov. Say you so?
  Indeed I have heard, 'tis fit a general
  Should not endanger his own person oft;
  So that he make a noise when he 's a-horseback,
  Like a Danske drummer,—Oh, 'tis excellent!—
  He need not fight! methinks his horse as well
  Might lead an army for him. If I live,
  I 'll charge the French foe in the very front
  Of all my troops, the foremost man.

Fran. What! what!

Giov. And will not bid my soldiers up, and follow,
  But bid them follow me.

Brach. Forward lapwing!
  He flies with the shell on 's head.

Fran. Pretty cousin!

Giov. The first year, uncle, that I go to war,
  All prisoners that I take, I will set free,
  Without their ransom.

Fran. Ha! without their ransom!
  How then will you reward your soldiers,
  That took those prisoners for you?

Giov. Thus, my lord:
  I 'll marry them to all the wealthy widows
  That falls that year.

Fran. Why then, the next year following,
  You 'll have no men to go with you to war.

Giov. Why then I 'll press the women to the war,
  And then the men will follow.

Mont. Witty prince!

Fran. See, a good habit makes a child a man,
  Whereas a bad one makes a man a beast.
  Come, you and I are friends.

Brach. Most wishedly:
  Like bones which, broke in sunder, and well set,
  Knit the more strongly.

Fran. Call Camillo hither.—
  You have receiv'd the rumour, how Count Lodowick
  Is turn'd a pirate?

Brach. Yes.

Fran. We are now preparing to fetch him in. Behold your duchess.
  We now will leave you, and expect from you
  Nothing but kind entreaty.

Brach. You have charm'd me.
                    [Exeunt Francisco, Monticelso, and Giovanni.
                        Enter Isabella
  You are in health, we see.

Isab. And above health,
  To see my lord well.

Brach. So: I wonder much
  What amorous whirlwind hurried you to Rome.

Isab. Devotion, my lord.

Brach. Devotion!
  Is your soul charg'd with any grievous sin?

Isab. 'Tis burden'd with too many; and I think
  The oftener that we cast our reckonings up,
  Our sleep will be the sounder.

Brach. Take your chamber.

Isab. Nay, my dear lord, I will not have you angry!
  Doth not my absence from you, now two months,
  Merit one kiss?

Brach. I do not use to kiss:
  If that will dispossess your jealousy,
  I 'll swear it to you.

Isab. O, my loved lord,
  I do not come to chide: my jealousy!
  I am to learn what that Italian means.
  You are as welcome to these longing arms,
  As I to you a virgin.

Brach. Oh, your breath!
  Out upon sweetmeats and continued physic,
  The plague is in them!

Isab. You have oft, for these two lips,
  Neglected cassia, or the natural sweets
  Of the spring-violet: they are not yet much wither'd.
  My lord, I should be merry: these your frowns
  Show in a helmet lovely; but on me,
  In such a peaceful interview, methinks
  They are too roughly knit.

Brach. O dissemblance!
  Do you bandy factions 'gainst me? have you learnt
  The trick of impudent baseness to complain
  Unto your kindred?

Isab. Never, my dear lord.

Brach. Must I be hunted out? or was 't your trick
  To meet some amorous gallant here in Rome,
  That must supply our discontinuance?

Isab. Pray, sir, burst my heart; and in my death
  Turn to your ancient pity, though not love.

Brach. Because your brother is the corpulent duke,
  That is, the great duke, 'sdeath, I shall not shortly
  Racket away five hundred crowns at tennis,
  But it shall rest 'pon record! I scorn him
  Like a shav'd Polack: all his reverend wit

Lies in his wardrobe; he 's a discreet fellow,
When he 's made up in his robes of state.
Your brother, the great duke, because h' 'as galleys,
And now and then ransacks a Turkish fly-boat,
(Now all the hellish furies take his soul!)
First made this match: accursed be the priest
That sang the wedding-mass, and even my issue!

Isab. Oh, too, too far you have curs'd!

Brach. Your hand I 'll kiss;
  This is the latest ceremony of my love.
  Henceforth I 'll never lie with thee; by this,
  This wedding-ring, I 'll ne'er more lie with thee!
  And this divorce shall be as truly kept,
  As if the judge had doomed it. Fare you well:
  Our sleeps are sever'd.

Isab. Forbid it the sweet union
  Of all things blessed! why, the saints in heaven
  Will knit their brows at that.

Brach. Let not thy love
  Make thee an unbeliever; this my vow
  Shall never, on my soul, be satisfied
  With my repentance: let thy brother rage
  Beyond a horrid tempest, or sea-fight,
  My vow is fixed.

Isab. O, my winding-sheet!
  Now shall I need thee shortly. Dear my lord,
  Let me hear once more, what I would not hear:
  Never?

Brach. Never.

Isab. Oh, my unkind lord! may your sins find mercy,
  As I upon a woeful widow'd bed
  Shall pray for you, if not to turn your eyes
  Upon your wretched wife and hopeful son,
  Yet that in time you 'll fix them upon heaven!

Brach. No more; go, go, complain to the great duke.

Isab. No, my dear lord; you shall have present witness
  How I 'll work peace between you. I will make
  Myself the author of your cursed vow;
  I have some cause to do it, you have none.
  Conceal it, I beseech you, for the weal
  Of both your dukedoms, that you wrought the means
  Of such a separation: let the fault
  Remain with my supposed jealousy,
  And think with what a piteous and rent heart
  I shall perform this sad ensuing part.

Enter Francisco, Flamineo, Monticelso, and Camillo

Brach. Well, take your course.—My honourable brother!

Fran. Sister!—This is not well, my lord.—Why, sister!—She merits not
  this welcome.

Brach. Welcome, say!
  She hath given a sharp welcome.

Fran. Are you foolish?
  Come, dry your tears: is this a modest course
  To better what is naught, to rail and weep?
  Grow to a reconcilement, or, by heaven,
  I 'll ne'er more deal between you.

Isab. Sir, you shall not;
  No, though Vittoria, upon that condition,
  Would become honest.

Fran. Was your husband loud
  Since we departed?

Isab. By my life, sir, no,
  I swear by that I do not care to lose.
  Are all these ruins of my former beauty
  Laid out for a whore's triumph?

Fran. Do you hear?
  Look upon other women, with what patience
  They suffer these slight wrongs, and with what justice
  They study to requite them: take that course.

Isab. O that I were a man, or that I had power
  To execute my apprehended wishes!
  I would whip some with scorpions.

Fran. What! turn'd fury!

Isab. To dig that strumpet's eyes out; let her lie
  Some twenty months a-dying; to cut off
  Her nose and lips, pull out her rotten teeth;
  Preserve her flesh like mummia, for trophies
  Of my just anger! Hell, to my affliction,
  Is mere snow-water. By your favour, sir;—
  Brother, draw near, and my lord cardinal;—
  Sir, let me borrow of you but one kiss;
  Henceforth I 'll never lie with you, by this,
  This wedding-ring.

Fran. How, ne'er more lie with him!

Isab. And this divorce shall be as truly kept
  As if in thronged court a thousand ears
  Had heard it, and a thousand lawyers' hands
  Sealed to the separation.

Brach. Ne'er lie with me!

Isab. Let not my former dotage
  Make thee an unbeliever; this my vow
  Shall never on my soul be satisfied
  With my repentance: manet alta mente repostum.

Fran. Now, by my birth, you are a foolish, mad,
  And jealous woman.

Brach. You see 'tis not my seeking.

Fran. Was this your circle of pure unicorn's horn,
  You said should charm your lord! now horns upon thee,
  For jealousy deserves them! Keep your vow
  And take your chamber.

Isab. No, sir, I 'll presently to Padua;
  I will not stay a minute.

Mont. Oh, good madam!

Brach. 'Twere best to let her have her humour;
  Some half-day's journey will bring down her stomach,
  And then she 'll turn in post.

Fran. To see her come
  To my lord for a dispensation
  Of her rash vow, will beget excellent laughter.

Isab. 'Unkindness, do thy office; poor heart, break:
  Those are the killing griefs, which dare not speak.' [Exit.

Marc. Camillo's come, my lord.

Enter Camillo

Fran. Where 's the commission?

Marc. 'Tis here.

Fran. Give me the signet.

Flam. [Leading Brachiano aside.] My lord, do you mark their whispering? I will compound a medicine, out of their two heads, stronger than garlic, deadlier than stibium: the cantharides, which are scarce seen to stick upon the flesh, when they work to the heart, shall not do it with more silence or invisible cunning.

Enter Doctor

Brach. About the murder?

Flam. They are sending him to Naples, but I 'll send him to Candy.
  Here 's another property too.

Brach. Oh, the doctor!

Flam. A poor quack-salving knave, my lord; one that should have been lashed for 's lechery, but that he confessed a judgment, had an execution laid upon him, and so put the whip to a non plus.

Doctor. And was cozened, my lord, by an arranter knave than myself, and made pay all the colorable execution.

Flam. He will shoot pills into a man's guts shall make them have more ventages than a cornet or a lamprey; he will poison a kiss; and was once minded for his masterpiece, because Ireland breeds no poison, to have prepared a deadly vapour in a Spaniard's fart, that should have poisoned all Dublin.

Brach. Oh, Saint Anthony's fire!

Doctor. Your secretary is merry, my lord.

Flam. O thou cursed antipathy to nature! Look, his eye 's bloodshot, like a needle a surgeon stitcheth a wound with. Let me embrace thee, toad, and love thee, O thou abominable, loathsome gargarism, that will fetch up lungs, lights, heart, and liver, by scruples!

Brach. No more.—I must employ thee, honest doctor:
  You must to Padua, and by the way,
  Use some of your skill for us.

Doctor. Sir, I shall.

Brach. But for Camillo?

Flam. He dies this night, by such a politic strain,
  Men shall suppose him by 's own engine slain.
  But for your duchess' death——

Doctor. I 'll make her sure.

Brach. Small mischiefs are by greater made secure.

Flam. Remember this, you slave; when knaves come to preferment, they
  rise as gallows in the Low Countries, one upon another's shoulders.
       [Exeunt. Monticelso, Camillo, and Francisco come forward.

Mont. Here is an emblem, nephew, pray peruse it:
  'Twas thrown in at your window.

Cam. At my window!
  Here is a stag, my lord, hath shed his horns,
  And, for the loss of them, the poor beast weeps:
  The word, Inopem me copia fecit.

Mont. That is,
  Plenty of horns hath made him poor of horns.

Cam. What should this mean?

Mont. I 'll tell you; 'tis given out
  You are a cuckold.

Cam. Is it given out so?
  I had rather such reports as that, my lord,
  Should keep within doors.

Fran. Have you any children?

Cam. None, my lord.

Fran. You are the happier:
  I 'll tell you a tale.

Cam. Pray, my lord.

Fran. An old tale.
  Upon a time Phbus, the god of light,
  Or him we call the sun, would need to be married:
  The gods gave their consent, and Mercury
  Was sent to voice it to the general world.
  But what a piteous cry there straight arose
  Amongst smiths and felt-makers, brewers and cooks,
  Reapers and butter-women, amongst fishmongers,
  And thousand other trades, which are annoyed
  By his excessive heat! 'twas lamentable.
  They came to Jupiter all in a sweat,
  And do forbid the banns. A great fat cook
  Was made their speaker, who entreats of Jove
  That Phbus might be gelded; for if now,
  When there was but one sun, so many men
  Were like to perish by his violent heat,
  What should they do if he were married,
  And should beget more, and those children
  Make fireworks like their father? So say I;
  Only I apply it to your wife;
  Her issue, should not providence prevent it,
  Would make both nature, time, and man repent it.

Mont. Look you, cousin,
  Go, change the air for shame; see if your absence
  Will blast your cornucopia. Marcello
  Is chosen with you joint commissioner,
  For the relieving our Italian coast
  From pirates.

Marc. I am much honour'd in 't.

Cam. But, sir,
  Ere I return, the stag's horns may be sprouted
  Greater than those are shed.

Mont. Do not fear it;
  I 'll be your ranger.

Cam. You must watch i' th' nights;
  Then 's the most danger.

Fran. Farewell, good Marcello:
  All the best fortunes of a soldier's wish
  Bring you a-shipboard.

Cam. Were I not best, now I am turn'd soldier,
  Ere that I leave my wife, sell all she hath,
  And then take leave of her?

Mont. I expect good from you,
  Your parting is so merry.

Cam. Merry, my lord! a' th' captain's humour right,
  I am resolved to be drunk this night. [Exeunt.

Fran. So, 'twas well fitted; now shall we discern
  How his wish'd absence will give violent way
  To Duke Brachiano's lust.

Mont. Why, that was it;
  To what scorn'd purpose else should we make choice
  Of him for a sea-captain? and, besides,
  Count Lodowick, which was rumour'd for a pirate,
  Is now in Padua.

Fran. Is 't true?

Mont. Most certain.
  I have letters from him, which are suppliant
  To work his quick repeal from banishment:
  He means to address himself for pension
  Unto our sister duchess.

Fran. Oh, 'twas well!
  We shall not want his absence past six days:
  I fain would have the Duke Brachiano run
  Into notorious scandal; for there 's naught

In such cursed dotage, to repair his name,
Only the deep sense of some deathless shame.

Mont. It may be objected, I am dishonourable
  To play thus with my kinsman; but I answer,
  For my revenge I 'd stake a brother's life,
  That being wrong'd, durst not avenge himself.

Fran. Come, to observe this strumpet.

Mont. Curse of greatness!
  Sure he 'll not leave her?

Fran. There 's small pity in 't:
  Like mistletoe on sere elms spent by weather,
  Let him cleave to her, and both rot together. [Exeunt.

SCENE II

Enter Brachiano, with one in the habit of a conjurer

Brach. Now, sir, I claim your promise: 'tis dead midnight,
  The time prefix'd to show me by your art,
  How the intended murder of Camillo,
  And our loath'd duchess, grow to action.

Conj. You have won me by your bounty to a deed
  I do not often practise. Some there are,
  Which by sophistic tricks, aspire that name
  Which I would gladly lose, of necromancer;
  As some that use to juggle upon cards,
  Seeming to conjure, when indeed they cheat;
  Others that raise up their confederate spirits
  'Bout windmills, and endanger their own necks
  For making of a squib; and some there are
  Will keep a curtal to show juggling tricks,
  And give out 'tis a spirit; besides these,
  Such a whole ream of almanac-makers, figure-flingers,
  Fellows, indeed that only live by stealth,
  Since they do merely lie about stol'n goods,
  They 'd make men think the devil were fast and loose,
  With speaking fustian Latin. Pray, sit down;
  Put on this nightcap, sir, 'tis charmed; and now
  I 'll show you, by my strong commanding art,
  The circumstance that breaks your duchess' heart.

A Dumb Show

Enter suspiciously Julio and Christophero: they draw a curtain where Brachiano's picture is; they put on spectacles of glass, which cover their eyes and noses, and then burn perfumes before the picture, and wash the lips of the picture; that done, quenching the fire, and putting off their spectacles, they depart laughing.

Enter Isabella in her night-gown, as to bedward, with lights, after her, Count Lodovico, Giovanni, Guidantonio, and others waiting on her: she kneels down as to prayers, then draws the curtain of the picture, does three reverences to it, and kisses it thrice; she faints, and will not suffer them to come near it; dies; sorrow expressed in Giovanni, and in Count Lodovico. She is conveyed out solemnly.

Brach. Excellent! then she 's dead.

Conj. She 's poisoned
  By the fumed picture. 'Twas her custom nightly,
  Before she went to bed, to go and visit
  Your picture, and to feed her eyes and lips
  On the dead shadow: Doctor Julio,
  Observing this, infects it with an oil,
  And other poison'd stuff, which presently
  Did suffocate her spirits.

Brach. Methought I saw
  Count Lodowick there.

Conj. He was; and by my art
  I find he did most passionately dote
  Upon your duchess. Now turn another way,
  And view Camillo's far more politic fate.
  Strike louder, music, from this charmed ground,
  To yield, as fits the act, a tragic sound!

The Second Dumb Show

Enter Flamineo, Marcello, Camillo, with four more as captains: they drink healths, and
dance; a vaulting horse is brought into the room; Marcello and two more whispered out of
the room, while Flamineo and Camillo strip themselves into their shirts, as to vault;
compliment who shall begin; as Camillo is about to vault, Flamineo pitcheth him upon his
neck, and, with the help of the rest, writhes his neck about; seems to see if it be broke, and
lays him folded double, as 'twere under the horse; makes show to call for help; Marcello
comes in, laments; sends for the cardinal and duke, who comes forth with armed men;
wonders at the act; commands the body to be carried home; apprehends Flamineo,
Marcello, and the rest, and go, as 'twere, to apprehend Vittoria.

Brach. 'Twas quaintly done; but yet each circumstance
  I taste not fully.

Conj. Oh, 'twas most apparent!
  You saw them enter, charg'd with their deep healths
  To their boon voyage; and, to second that,
  Flamineo calls to have a vaulting horse
  Maintain their sport; the virtuous Marcello
  Is innocently plotted forth the room;
  Whilst your eye saw the rest, and can inform you
  The engine of all.

Brach. It seems Marcello and Flamineo
  Are both committed.

31

Conj. Yes, you saw them guarded;
  And now they are come with purpose to apprehend
  Your mistress, fair Vittoria. We are now
  Beneath her roof: 'twere fit we instantly
  Make out by some back postern.

Brach. Noble friend,
  You bind me ever to you: this shall stand
  As the firm seal annexed to my hand;
  It shall enforce a payment. [Exit Brachiano.

Conj. Sir, I thank you.
  Both flowers and weeds spring, when the sun is warm,
  And great men do great good, or else great harm.
                    [Exit.

ACT III

SCENE I

Enter Francisco de Medicis, and Monticelso, their Chancellor and Register

Fran. You have dealt discreetly, to obtain the presence
  Of all the great lieger ambassadors
  To hear Vittoria's trial.

Mont. 'Twas not ill;
  For, sir, you know we have naught but circumstances
  To charge her with, about her husband's death:
  Their approbation, therefore, to the proofs
  Of her black lust shall make her infamous
  To all our neighbouring kingdoms. I wonder
  If Brachiano will be here?

Fran. Oh, fie! 'Twere impudence too palpable. [Exeunt.

Enter Flamineo and Marcello guarded, and a Lawyer

Lawyer. What, are you in by the week? So—I will try now whether they
  wit be close prisoner—methinks none should sit upon thy sister, but
  old whore-masters——

Flam. Or cuckolds; for your cuckold is your most terrible tickler of
  lechery. Whore-masters would serve; for none are judges at tilting,
  but those that have been old tilters.

Lawyer. My lord duke and she have been very private.

Flam. You are a dull ass; 'tis threatened they have been very public.

Lawyer. If it can be proved they have but kissed one another——

Flam. What then?

Lawyer. My lord cardinal will ferret them.

Flam. A cardinal, I hope, will not catch conies.

Lawyer. For to sow kisses (mark what I say), to sow kisses is to reap
  lechery; and, I am sure, a woman that will endure kissing is half won.

Flam. True, her upper part, by that rule; if you will win her neither
  part too, you know what follows.

Lawyer. Hark! the ambassadors are 'lighted——

Flam. I do put on this feigned garb of mirth,
  To gull suspicion.

Marc. Oh, my unfortunate sister!
  I would my dagger-point had cleft her heart
  When she first saw Brachiano: you, 'tis said,
  Were made his engine, and his stalking horse,
  To undo my sister.

Flam. I am a kind of path
  To her and mine own preferment.

Marc. Your ruin.

Flam. Hum! thou art a soldier,
  Followest the great duke, feed'st his victories,
  As witches do their serviceable spirits,
  Even with thy prodigal blood: what hast got?
  But, like the wealth of captains, a poor handful,
  Which in thy palm thou bear'st, as men hold water;
  Seeking to grip it fast, the frail reward
  Steals through thy fingers.

Marc. Sir!

Flam. Thou hast scarce maintenance
  To keep thee in fresh chamois.

Marc. Brother!

Flam. Hear me:
  And thus, when we have even pour'd ourselves
  Into great fights, for their ambition,
  Or idle spleen, how shall we find reward?
  But as we seldom find the mistletoe,
  Sacred to physic, on the builder oak,
  Without a mandrake by it; so in our quest of gain,
  Alas, the poorest of their forc'd dislikes
  At a limb proffers, but at heart it strikes!
  This is lamented doctrine.

Marc. Come, come.

Flam. When age shall turn thee
  White as a blooming hawthorn——

Marc. I 'll interrupt you:
  For love of virtue bear an honest heart,
  And stride o'er every politic respect,
  Which, where they most advance, they most infect.
  Were I your father, as I am your brother,
  I should not be ambitious to leave you
  A better patrimony.

Flam. I 'll think on 't. [Enter Savoy Ambassador.
  The lord ambassadors.

[Here there is a passage of the Lieger Ambassadors over the stage
  severally.

Enter French Ambassador

Lawyer. Oh, my sprightly Frenchman! Do you know him? he 's an admirable tilter.

Flam. I saw him at last tilting: he showed like a pewter candlestick fashioned like a man in armour, holding a tilting staff in his hand, little bigger than a candle of twelve i' th' pound.

Lawyer. Oh, but he's an excellent horseman!

Flam. A lame one in his lofty tricks; he sleeps a-horseback, like a poulterer.

Enter English and Spanish

Lawyer. Lo you, my Spaniard!

Flam. He carried his face in 's ruff, as I have seen a serving-man carry glasses in a cypress hatband, monstrous steady, for fear of breaking; he looks like the claw of a blackbird, first salted, and then broiled in a candle. [Exeunt.

SCENE II

The Arraignment of Vittoria

Enter Francisco, Monticelso, the six Lieger Ambassadors, Brachiano,
  Vittoria, Zanche, Flamineo, Marcello, Lawyer, and a Guard.

Mont. Forbear, my lord, here is no place assign'd you.
  This business, by his Holiness, is left
  To our examination.

Brach. May it thrive with you. [Lays a rich gown under him.

Fran. A chair there for his Lordship.

Brach. Forbear your kindness: an unbidden guest
  Should travel as Dutch women go to church,
  Bear their stools with them.

Mont. At your pleasure, sir.
  Stand to the table, gentlewoman. Now, signior,
  Fall to your plea.

Lawyer. Domine judex, converte oculos in hanc pestem, mulierum
  corruptissiman.

Vit. What 's he?

Fran. A lawyer that pleads against you.

Vit. Pray, my lord, let him speak his usual tongue,
  I 'll make no answer else.

Fran. Why, you understand Latin.

Vit. I do, sir, but amongst this auditory
  Which come to hear my cause, the half or more
  May be ignorant in 't.

Mont. Go on, sir.

Vit. By your favour,
  I will not have my accusation clouded
  In a strange tongue: all this assembly
  Shall hear what you can charge me with.

Fran. Signior,
  You need not stand on 't much; pray, change your language.

Mont. Oh, for God's sake—Gentlewoman, your credit
  Shall be more famous by it.

Lawyer. Well then, have at you.

Vit. I am at the mark, sir; I 'll give aim to you,
  And tell you how near you shoot.

Lawyer. Most literated judges, please your lordships
  So to connive your judgments to the view
  Of this debauch'd and diversivolent woman;
  Who such a black concatenation
  Of mischief hath effected, that to extirp
  The memory of 't, must be the consummation
  Of her, and her projections——

Vit. What 's all this?

Lawyer. Hold your peace!
  Exorbitant sins must have exulceration.

Vit. Surely, my lords, this lawyer here hath swallow'd
  Some 'pothecaries' bills, or proclamations;
  And now the hard and undigestible words
  Come up, like stones we use give hawks for physic.
  Why, this is Welsh to Latin.

Lawyer. My lords, the woman
  Knows not her tropes, nor figures, nor is perfect
  In the academic derivation
  Of grammatical elocution.

Fran. Sir, your pains
  Shall be well spar'd, and your deep eloquence
  Be worthily applauded amongst thouse
  Which understand you.

Lawyer. My good lord.

Fran. Sir,
  Put up your papers in your fustian bag—
                    [Francisco speaks this as in scorn.

37

Cry mercy, sir, 'tis buckram and accept
My notion of your learn'd verbosity.

Lawyer. I most graduatically thank your lordship:
 I shall have use for them elsewhere.

Mont. I shall be plainer with you, and paint out
 Your follies in more natural red and white
 Than that upon your cheek.

Vit. Oh, you mistake!
 You raise a blood as noble in this cheek
 As ever was your mother's.

Mont. I must spare you, till proof cry whore to that.
 Observe this creature here, my honour'd lords,
 A woman of most prodigious spirit,
 In her effected.

Vit. My honourable lord,
 It doth not suit a reverend cardinal
 To play the lawyer thus.

Mont. Oh, your trade instructs your language!
 You see, my lords, what goodly fruit she seems;
 Yet like those apples travellers report
 To grow where Sodom and Gomorrah stood,
 I will but touch her, and you straight shall see
 She 'll fall to soot and ashes.

Vit. Your envenom'd 'pothecary should do 't.

Mont. I am resolv'd,
 Were there a second paradise to lose,
 This devil would betray it.

Vit. O poor Charity!
 Thou art seldom found in scarlet.

Mont. Who knows not how, when several night by night
 Her gates were chok'd with coaches, and her rooms
 Outbrav'd the stars with several kind of lights;
 When she did counterfeit a prince's court
 In music, banquets, and most riotous surfeits;
 This whore forsooth was holy.

Vit. Ha! whore! what 's that?

Mont. Shall I expound whore to you? sure I shall;
  I 'll give their perfect character. They are first,
  Sweetmeats which rot the eater; in man's nostrils
  Poison'd perfumes. They are cozening alchemy;
  Shipwrecks in calmest weather. What are whores!
  Cold Russian winters, that appear so barren,
  As if that nature had forgot the spring.
  They are the true material fire of hell:
  Worse than those tributes i' th' Low Countries paid,
  Exactions upon meat, drink, garments, sleep,
  Ay, even on man's perdition, his sin.
  They are those brittle evidences of law,
  Which forfeit all a wretched man's estate
  For leaving out one syllable. What are whores!
  They are those flattering bells have all one tune,
  At weddings, and at funerals. Your rich whores
  Are only treasuries by extortion fill'd,
  And emptied by curs'd riot. They are worse,
  Worse than dead bodies which are begg'd at gallows,
  And wrought upon by surgeons, to teach man
  Wherein he is imperfect. What's a whore!
  She 's like the guilty counterfeited coin,
  Which, whosoe'er first stamps it, brings in trouble
  All that receive it.

Vit. This character 'scapes me.

Mont. You, gentlewoman!
  Take from all beasts and from all minerals
  Their deadly poison——

Vit. Well, what then?

Mont. I 'll tell thee;
  I 'll find in thee a 'pothecary's shop,
  To sample them all.

Fr. Ambass. She hath liv'd ill.

Eng. Ambass. True, but the cardinal 's too bitter.

Mont. You know what whore is. Next the devil adultery,
  Enters the devil murder.

Fran. Your unhappy husband
  Is dead.

Vit. Oh, he 's a happy husband!
  Now he owes nature nothing.

Fran. And by a vaulting engine.

Mont. An active plot; he jump'd into his grave.

Fran. What a prodigy was 't,
  That from some two yards' height, a slender man
  Should break his neck!

Mont. I' th' rushes!

Fran. And what's more,
  Upon the instant lose all use of speech,
  All vital motion, like a man had lain
  Wound up three days. Now mark each circumstance.

Mont. And look upon this creature was his wife!
  She comes not like a widow; she comes arm'd
  With scorn and impudence: is this a mourning-habit?

Vit. Had I foreknown his death, as you suggest,
  I would have bespoke my mourning.

Mont. Oh, you are cunning!

Vit. You shame your wit and judgment,
  To call it so. What! is my just defence
  By him that is my judge call'd impudence?
  Let me appeal then from this Christian court,
  To the uncivil Tartar.

Mont. See, my lords,
  She scandals our proceedings.

Vit. Humbly thus,
  Thus low to the most worthy and respected
  Lieger ambassadors, my modesty
  And womanhood I tender; but withal,
  So entangled in a curs'd accusation,
  That my defence, of force, like Perseus,
  Must personate masculine virtue. To the point.

Find me but guilty, sever head from body,
We 'll part good friends: I scorn to hold my life
At yours, or any man's entreaty, sir.

Eng. Ambass. She hath a brave spirit.

Mont. Well, well, such counterfeit jewels
 Make true ones oft suspected.

Vit. You are deceiv'd:
 For know, that all your strict-combined heads,
 Which strike against this mine of diamonds,
 Shall prove but glassen hammers: they shall break.
 These are but feigned shadows of my evils.
 Terrify babes, my lord, with painted devils,
 I am past such needless palsy. For your names
 Of 'whore' and 'murderess', they proceed from you,
 As if a man should spit against the wind,
 The filth returns in 's face.

Mont. Pray you, mistress, satisfy me one question:
 Who lodg'd beneath your roof that fatal night
 Your husband broke his neck?

Brach. That question
 Enforceth me break silence: I was there.

Mont. Your business?

Brach. Why, I came to comfort her,
 And take some course for settling her estate,
 Because I heard her husband was in debt
 To you, my lord.

Mont. He was.

Brach. And 'twas strangely fear'd,
 That you would cozen her.

Mont. Who made you overseer?

Brach. Why, my charity, my charity, which should flow
 From every generous and noble spirit,
 To orphans and to widows.

Mont. Your lust!

Brach. Cowardly dogs bark loudest: sirrah priest,
  I 'll talk with you hereafter. Do you hear?
  The sword you frame of such an excellent temper,
  I 'll sheath in your own bowels.
  There are a number of thy coat resemble
  Your common post-boys.

Mont. Ha!

Brach. Your mercenary post-boys;
  Your letters carry truth, but 'tis your guise
  To fill your mouths with gross and impudent lies.

Servant. My lord, your gown.

Brach. Thou liest, 'twas my stool:
  Bestow 't upon thy master, that will challenge
  The rest o' th' household-stuff; for Brachiano
  Was ne'er so beggarly to take a stool
  Out of another's lodging: let him make
  Vallance for his bed on 't, or a demy foot-cloth
  For his most reverend moil. Monticelso,
  Nemo me impune lacessit. [Exit.

Mont. Your champion's gone.

Vit. The wolf may prey the better.

Fran. My lord, there 's great suspicion of the murder,
  But no sound proof who did it. For my part,
  I do not think she hath a soul so black
  To act a deed so bloody; if she have,
  As in cold countries husbandmen plant vines,
  And with warm blood manure them; even so
  One summer she will bear unsavoury fruit,
  And ere next spring wither both branch and root.
  The act of blood let pass; only descend
  To matters of incontinence.

Vit. I discern poison
  Under your gilded pills.

Mont. Now the duke's gone, I will produce a letter
  Wherein 'twas plotted, he and you should meet
  At an apothecary's summer-house,

42

Down by the River Tiber,—view 't, my lords,
Where after wanton bathing and the heat
Of a lascivious banquet—I pray read it,
I shame to speak the rest.

Vit. Grant I was tempted;
  Temptation to lust proves not the act:
  Casta est quam nemo rogavit.
  You read his hot love to me, but you want
  My frosty answer.

Mont. Frost i' th' dog-days! strange!

Vit. Condemn you me for that the duke did love me?
  So may you blame some fair and crystal river,
  For that some melancholic distracted man
  Hath drown'd himself in 't.

Mont. Truly drown'd, indeed.

Vit. Sum up my faults, I pray, and you shall find,
  That beauty and gay clothes, a merry heart,
  And a good stomach to feast, are all,
  All the poor crimes that you can charge me with.
  In faith, my lord, you might go pistol flies,
  The sport would be more noble.

Mont. Very good.

Vit. But take your course: it seems you 've beggar'd me first,
  And now would fain undo me. I have houses,
  Jewels, and a poor remnant of crusadoes;
  Would those would make you charitable!

Mont. If the devil
  Did ever take good shape, behold his picture.

Vit. You have one virtue left,
  You will not flatter me.

Fran. Who brought this letter?

Vit. I am not compell'd to tell you.

Mont. My lord duke sent to you a thousand ducats
  The twelfth of August.

43

Vit. 'Twas to keep your cousin
  From prison; I paid use for 't.

Mont. I rather think,
  'Twas interest for his lust.

Vit. Who says so but yourself?
  If you be my accuser,
  Pray cease to be my judge: come from the bench;
  Give in your evidence 'gainst me, and let these
  Be moderators. My lord cardinal,
  Were your intelligencing ears as loving
  As to my thoughts, had you an honest tongue,
  I would not care though you proclaim'd them all.

Mont. Go to, go to.
  After your goodly and vainglorious banquet,
  I 'll give you a choke-pear.

Vit. O' your own grafting?

Mont. You were born in Venice, honourably descended
  From the Vittelli: 'twas my cousin's fate,
  Ill may I name the hour, to marry you;
  He bought you of your father.

Vit. Ha!

Mont. He spent there in six months
  Twelve thousand ducats, and (to my acquaintance)
  Receiv'd in dowry with you not one Julio:
  'Twas a hard pennyworth, the ware being so light.
  I yet but draw the curtain; now to your picture:
  You came from thence a most notorious strumpet,
  And so you have continued.

Vit. My lord!

Mont. Nay, hear me,
  You shall have time to prate. My Lord Brachiano—
  Alas! I make but repetition
  Of what is ordinary and Rialto talk,
  And ballated, and would be play'd a' th' stage,
  But that vice many times finds such loud friends,
  That preachers are charm'd silent.

You, gentlemen, Flamineo and Marcello,
The Court hath nothing now to charge you with,
Only you must remain upon your sureties
For your appearance.

Fran. I stand for Marcello.

Flam. And my lord duke for me.

Mont. For you, Vittoria, your public fault,
   Join'd to th' condition of the present time,
   Takes from you all the fruits of noble pity,
   Such a corrupted trial have you made
   Both of your life and beauty, and been styl'd
   No less an ominous fate than blazing stars
   To princes. Hear your sentence: you are confin'd
   Unto a house of convertites, and your bawd——

Flam. [Aside.] Who, I?

Mont. The Moor.

Flam. [Aside.] Oh, I am a sound man again.

Vit. A house of convertites! what 's that?

Mont. A house of penitent whores.

Vit. Do the noblemen in Rome
   Erect it for their wives, that I am sent
   To lodge there?

Fran. You must have patience.

Vit. I must first have vengeance!
   I fain would know if you have your salvation
   By patent, that you proceed thus.

Mont. Away with her,
   Take her hence.

Vit. A rape! a rape!

Mont. How?

Vit. Yes, you have ravish'd justice;
  Forc'd her to do your pleasure.

Mont. Fie, she 's mad——

Vit. Die with those pills in your most cursed maw,
  Should bring you health! or while you sit o' th' bench,
  Let your own spittle choke you!

Mont. She 's turned fury.

Vit. That the last day of judgment may so find you,
  And leave you the same devil you were before!
  Instruct me, some good horse-leech, to speak treason;
  For since you cannot take my life for deeds,
  Take it for words. O woman's poor revenge,
  Which dwells but in the tongue! I will not weep;
  No, I do scorn to call up one poor tear
  To fawn on your injustice: bear me hence
  Unto this house of—what's your mitigating title?

Mont. Of convertites.

Vit. It shall not be a house of convertites;
  My mind shall make it honester to me
  Than the Pope's palace, and more peaceable
  Than thy soul, though thou art a cardinal.
  Know this, and let it somewhat raise your spite,
  Through darkness diamonds spread their richest light. [Exit.

Enter Brachiano

Brach. Now you and I are friends, sir, we'll shake hands
  In a friend's grave together; a fit place,
  Being th' emblem of soft peace, t' atone our hatred.

Fran. Sir, what 's the matter?

Brach. I will not chase more blood from that lov'd cheek;
  You have lost too much already; fare you well. [Exit.

Fran. How strange these words sound! what 's the interpretation?

Flam. [Aside.] Good; this is a preface to the discovery of the duchess' death: he carries it well. Because now I cannot counterfeit a whining passion for the death of my lady, I will feign a mad humour for the disgrace of my sister; and that will keep off idle questions.

46

Treason's tongue hath a villainous palsy in 't; I will talk to any man, hear no man, and for a time appear a politic madman.

Enter Giovanni, and Count Lodovico

Fran. How now, my noble cousin? what, in black!

Giov. Yes, uncle, I was taught to imitate you
  In virtue, and you must imitate me
  In colours of your garments. My sweet mother
  Is——

Fran. How? where?

Giov. Is there; no, yonder: indeed, sir, I 'll not tell you,
  For I shall make you weep.

Fran. Is dead?

Giov. Do not blame me now,
  I did not tell you so.

Lodo. She 's dead, my lord.

Fran. Dead!

Mont. Bless'd lady, thou art now above thy woes!
  Will 't please your lordships to withdraw a little?

Giov. What do the dead do, uncle? do they eat,
  Hear music, go a-hunting, and be merry,
  As we that live?

Fran. No, coz; they sleep.

Giov. Lord, Lord, that I were dead!
  I have not slept these six nights. When do they wake?

Fran. When God shall please.

Giov. Good God, let her sleep ever!
  For I have known her wake an hundred nights,
  When all the pillow where she laid her head
  Was brine-wet with her tears. I am to complain to you, sir;
  I 'll tell you how they have us'd her now she 's dead:

They wrapp'd her in a cruel fold of lead,
And would not let me kiss her.

Fran. Thou didst love her?

Giov. I have often heard her say she gave me suck,
  And it should seem by that she dearly lov'd me,
  Since princes seldom do it.

Fran. Oh, all of my poor sister that remains!
  Take him away for God's sake! [Exit Giovanni.

Mont. How now, my lord?

Fran. Believe me, I am nothing but her grave;
  And I shall keep her blessed memory
  Longer than thousand epitaphs.

SCENE III

Enter Flamineo as distracted, Marcello, and Lodovico

Flam. We endure the strokes like anvils or hard steel, Till pain itself make us no pain to feel. Who shall do me right now? is this the end of service? I'd rather go weed garlic; travail through France, and be mine own ostler; wear sheep-skin linings, or shoes that stink of blacking; be entered into the list of the forty thousand pedlars in Poland. [Enter Savoy Ambassador.] Would I had rotted in some surgeon's house at Venice, built upon the pox as well as on piles, ere I had served Brachiano!

Savoy Ambass. You must have comfort.

Flam. Your comfortable words are like honey: they relish well in your mouth that 's whole, but in mine that 's wounded, they go down as if the sting of the bee were in them. Oh, they have wrought their purpose cunningly, as if they would not seem to do it of malice! In this a politician imitates the devil, as the devil imitates a canon; wheresoever he comes to do mischief, he comes with his backside towards you.

Enter French Ambassador

Fr. Ambass. The proofs are evident.

Flam. Proof! 'twas corruption. O gold, what a god art thou! and O man, what a devil art thou to be tempted by that cursed mineral! Your diversivolent lawyer, mark him! knaves turn informers, as maggots turn to flies, you may catch gudgeons with either. A cardinal! I would he would hear me: there 's nothing so holy but money will corrupt and putrify it, like victual under the line. [Enter English Ambassador.] You are happy in England, my lord; here they sell justice with those weights they press men to death with. O horrible salary!

Eng. Ambass. Fie, fie, Flamineo.

Flam. Bells ne'er ring well, till they are at their full pitch; and I hope yon cardinal shall never have the grace to pray well, till he come to the scaffold. If they were racked now to know the confederacy: but your noblemen are privileged from the rack; and well may, for a little thing would pull some of them a-pieces afore they came to their arraignment. Religion, oh, how it is commeddled with policy! The first blood shed in the world happened about religion. Would I were a Jew!

Marc. Oh, there are too many!

Flam. You are deceived; there are not Jews enough, priests enough, nor gentlemen enough.

Marc. How?

Flam. I 'll prove it; for if there were Jews enough, so many Christians would not turn usurers; if priests enough, one should not have six benefices; and if gentlemen enough, so many early mushrooms, whose best growth sprang from a live by begging: be thou one of them practise the art of Wolner in England, to swallow all 's given thee: and yet let one purgation make thee as hungry again as fellows that work in a saw-pit. I 'll go hear the screech-owl. [Exit.

Lodo. This was Brachiano's pander; and 'tis strange
  That in such open, and apparent guilt
  Of his adulterous sister, he dare utter
  So scandalous a passion. I must wind him.

Re-enter Flamineo.

Flam. How dares this banish'd count return to Rome,
  His pardon not yet purchas'd! I have heard
  The deceased duchess gave him pension,
  And that he came along from Padua
  I' th' train of the young prince. There 's somewhat in 't:
  Physicians, that cure poisons, still do work
  With counter-poisons.

Marc. Mark this strange encounter.

Flam. The god of melancholy turn thy gall to poison,
  And let the stigmatic wrinkles in thy face,
  Like to the boisterous waves in a rough tide,
  One still overtake another.

Lodo. I do thank thee,
  And I do wish ingeniously for thy sake,
  The dog-days all year long.

Flam. How croaks the raven?
  Is our good duchess dead?

Lodo. Dead.

Flam. O fate!
  Misfortune comes like the coroner's business
  Huddle upon huddle.

Lodo. Shalt thou and I join housekeeping?

Flam. Yes, content:
  Let 's be unsociably sociable.

Lodo. Sit some three days together, and discourse?

Flam. Only with making faces;
  Lie in our clothes.

Lodo. With faggots for our pillows.

Flam. And be lousy.

Lodo. In taffeta linings, that 's genteel melancholy;
  Sleep all day.

Flam. Yes; and, like your melancholic hare,
  Feed after midnight. [Enter Antonelli and Gasparo.
  We are observed: see how yon couple grieve.

Lodo. What a strange creature is a laughing fool!
  As if man were created to no use
  But only to show his teeth.

Flam. I 'll tell thee what,
  It would do well instead of looking-glasses,
  To set one's face each morning by a saucer
  Of a witch's congeal'd blood.

Lodo. Precious rogue!
  We'll never part.

Flam. Never, till the beggary of courtiers,
  The discontent of churchmen, want of soldiers,
  And all the creatures that hang manacled,
  Worse than strappadoed, on the lowest felly
  Of fortune's wheel, be taught, in our two lives,
  To scorn that world which life of means deprives.

Ant. My lord, I bring good news. The Pope, on 's death bed,
  At th' earnest suit of the great Duke of Florence,
  Hath sign'd your pardon, and restor'd unto you——

Lodo. I thank you for your news. Look up again,
  Flamineo, see my pardon.

Flam. Why do you laugh?
  There was no such condition in our covenant.

Lodo. Why?

Flam. You shall not seem a happier man than I:
  You know our vow, sir; if you will be merry,
  Do it i' th' like posture, as if some great man
  Sat while his enemy were executed:
  Though it be very lechery unto thee,
  Do 't with a crabbed politician's face.

Lodo. Your sister is a damnable whore.

Flam. Ha!

Lodo. Look you, I spake that laughing.

Flam. Dost ever think to speak again?

Lodo. Do you hear?
  Wilt sell me forty ounces of her blood
  To water a mandrake?

Flam. Poor lord, you did vow
  To live a lousy creature.

Lodo. Yes.

Flam. Like one
  That had for ever forfeited the daylight,
  By being in debt.

Lodo. Ha, ha!

Flam. I do not greatly wonder you do break,
  Your lordship learn'd 't long since. But I 'll tell you.

Lodo. What?

Flam. And 't shall stick by you.

Lodo. I long for it.

Flam. This laughter scurvily becomes your face:
  If you will not be melancholy, be angry. [Strikes him.
  See, now I laugh too.

Marc. You are to blame: I 'll force you hence.

52

Lodo. Unhand me. [Exeunt Marcello and Flamineo.
  That e'er I should be forc'd to right myself,
  Upon a pander!

Ant. My lord.

Lodo. H' had been as good met with his fist a thunderbolt.

Gas. How this shows!

Lodo. Ud's death! how did my sword miss him?
  These rogues that are most weary of their lives
  Still 'scape the greatest dangers.
  A pox upon him; all his reputation,
  Nay, all the goodness of his family,
  Is not worth half this earthquake:
  I learn'd it of no fencer to shake thus:
  Come, I 'll forget him, and go drink some wine.
                              [Exeunt.

ACT IV

SCENE I

Enter Francisco and Monticelso

Mont. Come, come, my lord, untie your folded thoughts,
  And let them dangle loose, as a bride's hair.
  Your sister's poisoned.

Fran. Far be it from my thoughts
  To seek revenge.

Mont. What, are you turn'd all marble?

Fran. Shall I defy him, and impose a war,
  Most burthensome on my poor subjects' necks,
  Which at my will I have not power to end?
  You know, for all the murders, rapes, and thefts,
  Committed in the horrid lust of war,
  He that unjustly caus'd it first proceed,
  Shall find it in his grave, and in his seed.

Mont. That 's not the course I 'd wish you; pray observe me.
  We see that undermining more prevails
  Than doth the cannon. Bear your wrongs conceal'd,
  And, patient as the tortoise, let this camel
  Stalk o'er your back unbruis'd: sleep with the lion,
  And let this brood of secure foolish mice
  Play with your nostrils, till the time be ripe
  For th' bloody audit, and the fatal gripe:
  Aim like a cunning fowler, close one eye,
  That you the better may your game espy.

Fran. Free me, my innocence, from treacherous acts!
  I know there 's thunder yonder; and I 'll stand,
  Like a safe valley, which low bends the knee
  To some aspiring mountain: since I know
  Treason, like spiders weaving nets for flies,
  By her foul work is found, and in it dies.
  To pass away these thoughts, my honour'd lord,
  It is reported you possess a book,
  Wherein you have quoted, by intelligence,
  The names of all notorious offenders
  Lurking about the city.

Mont. Sir, I do;
  And some there are which call it my black-book.
  Well may the title hold; for though it teach not
  The art of conjuring, yet in it lurk
  The names of many devils.

Fran. Pray let 's see it.

Mont. I 'll fetch it to your lordship. [Exit.

Fran. Monticelso,
  I will not trust thee, but in all my plots
  I 'll rest as jealous as a town besieg'd.
  Thou canst not reach what I intend to act:
  Your flax soon kindles, soon is out again,
  But gold slow heats, and long will hot remain.

Enter Monticelso, with the book

Mont. 'Tis here, my lord.

Fran. First, your intelligencers, pray let 's see.

Mont. Their number rises strangely;
  And some of them
  You 'd take for honest men.
  Next are panders.
  These are your pirates; and these following leaves
  For base rogues, that undo young gentlemen,
  By taking up commodities; for politic bankrupts;
  For fellows that are bawds to their own wives,
  Only to put off horses, and slight jewels,
  Clocks, defac'd plate, and such commodities,
  At birth of their first children.

Fran. Are there such?

Mont. These are for impudent bawds,
  That go in men's apparel; for usurers
  That share with scriveners for their good reportage:
  For lawyers that will antedate their writs:
  And some divines you might find folded there,
  But that I slip them o'er for conscience' sake.
  Here is a general catalogue of knaves:

A man might study all the prisons o'er,
Yet never attain this knowledge.

Fran. Murderers?
   Fold down the leaf, I pray;
   Good my lord, let me borrow this strange doctrine.

Mont. Pray, use 't, my lord.

Fran. I do assure your lordship,
   You are a worthy member of the State,
   And have done infinite good in your discovery
   Of these offenders.

Mont. Somewhat, sir.

Fran. O God!
   Better than tribute of wolves paid in England;
   'Twill hang their skins o' th' hedge.

Mont. I must make bold
   To leave your lordship.

Fran. Dearly, sir, I thank you:
   If any ask for me at court, report
   You have left me in the company of knaves.
                              [Exit Monticelso.
   I gather now by this, some cunning fellow
   That 's my lord's officer, and that lately skipp'd
   From a clerk's desk up to a justice' chair,
   Hath made this knavish summons, and intends,
   As th' Irish rebels wont were to sell heads,
   So to make prize of these. And thus it happens:
   Your poor rogues pay for 't, which have not the means
   To present bribe in fist; the rest o' th' band
   Are razed out of the knaves' record; or else
   My lord he winks at them with easy will;
   His man grows rich, the knaves are the knaves still.
   But to the use I 'll make of it; it shall serve
   To point me out a list of murderers,
   Agents for my villany. Did I want
   Ten leash of courtesans, it would furnish me;
   Nay, laundress three armies. That in so little paper
   Should lie th' undoing of so many men!
   'Tis not so big as twenty declarations.

See the corrupted use some make of books:
Divinity, wrested by some factious blood,
Draws swords, swells battles, and o'erthrows all good.
To fashion my revenge more seriously,
Let me remember my dear sister's face:
Call for her picture? no, I 'll close mine eyes,
And in a melancholic thought I 'll frame
                    [Enter Isabella's Ghost.
Her figure 'fore me. Now I ha' 't—how strong
Imagination works! how she can frame
Things which are not! methinks she stands afore me,
And by the quick idea of my mind,
Were my skill pregnant, I could draw her picture.
Thought, as a subtle juggler, makes us deem
Things supernatural, which have cause
Common as sickness. 'Tis my melancholy.
How cam'st thou by thy death?—how idle am I
To question mine own idleness!—did ever
Man dream awake till now?—remove this object;
Out of my brain with 't: what have I to do
With tombs, or death-beds, funerals, or tears,
That have to meditate upon revenge? [Exit Ghost.
So, now 'tis ended, like an old wife's story.
Statesmen think often they see stranger sights
Than madmen. Come, to this weighty business.
My tragedy must have some idle mirth in 't,
Else it will never pass. I am in love,
In love with Corombona; and my suit
Thus halts to her in verse.— [He writes.
I have done it rarely: Oh, the fate of princes!
I am so us'd to frequent flattery,
That, being alone, I now flatter myself:
But it will serve; 'tis seal'd. [Enter servant.] Bear this
To the House of Convertites, and watch your leisure
To give it to the hands of Corombona,
Or to the Matron, when some followers
Of Brachiano may be by. Away! [Exit Servant.
He that deals all by strength, his wit is shallow;
When a man's head goes through, each limb will follow.
The engine for my business, bold Count Lodowick;
'Tis gold must such an instrument procure,
With empty fist no man doth falcons lure.
Brachiano, I am now fit for thy encounter:

Like the wild Irish, I 'll ne'er think thee dead
Till I can play at football with thy head,
Flectere si nequeo superos, Acheronta movebo. [Exit.

SCENE II

Enter the Matron, and Flamineo

Matron. Should it be known the duke hath such recourse
  To your imprison'd sister, I were like
  T' incur much damage by it.

Flam. Not a scruple.
  The Pope lies on his death-bed, and their heads
  Are troubled now with other business
  Than guarding of a lady.

Enter Servant

Servant. Yonder 's Flamineo in conference
  With the Matrona.—Let me speak with you:
  I would entreat you to deliver for me
  This letter to the fair Vittoria.

Matron. I shall, sir.

Enter Brachiano

Servant. With all care and secrecy;
  Hereafter you shall know me, and receive
  Thanks for this courtesy. [Exit.

Flam. How now? what 's that?

Matron. A letter.

Flam. To my sister? I 'll see 't deliver'd.

Brach. What 's that you read, Flamineo?

Flam. Look.

Brach. Ha! 'To the most unfortunate, his best respected Vittoria'.
  Who was the messenger?

Flam. I know not.

Brach. No! who sent it?

Flam. Ud's foot! you speak as if a man
  Should know what fowl is coffin'd in a bak'd meat
  Afore you cut it up.

Brach. I 'll open 't, were 't her heart. What 's here subscrib'd!
  Florence! this juggling is gross and palpable.
  I have found out the conveyance. Read it, read it.

Flam. [Reads the letter.] "Your tears I 'll turn to triumphs, be but
  mine;
  Your prop is fallen: I pity, that a vine
  Which princes heretofore have long'd to gather,
  Wanting supporters, now should fade and wither."
  Wine, i' faith, my lord, with lees would serve his turn.
  "Your sad imprisonment I 'll soon uncharm,
  And with a princely uncontrolled arm
  Lead you to Florence, where my love and care
  Shall hang your wishes in my silver hair."
  A halter on his strange equivocation!
  "Nor for my years return me the sad willow;
  Who prefer blossoms before fruit that 's mellow?"
  Rotten, on my knowledge, with lying too long i' th' bedstraw.
  "And all the lines of age this line convinces;
  The gods never wax old, no more do princes."
  A pox on 't, tear it; let 's have no more atheists, for God's sake.

Brach. Ud's death! I 'll cut her into atomies,
  And let th' irregular north wind sweep her up,
  And blow her int' his nostrils: where 's this whore?

Flam. What? what do you call her?

Brach. Oh, I could be mad!
  Prevent the curs'd disease she 'll bring me to,
  And tear my hair off. Where 's this changeable stuff?

Flam. O'er head and ears in water, I assure you;
  She is not for your wearing.

Brach. In, you pander!

Flam. What, me, my lord? am I your dog?

Brach. A bloodhound: do you brave, do you stand me?

60

Flam. Stand you! let those that have diseases run;
  I need no plasters.

Brach. Would you be kick'd?

Flam. Would you have your neck broke?
  I tell you, duke, I am not in Russia;
  My shins must be kept whole.

Brach. Do you know me?

Flam. Oh, my lord, methodically!
  As in this world there are degrees of evils,
  So in this world there are degrees of devils.
  You 're a great duke, I your poor secretary.
  I do look now for a Spanish fig, or an Italian sallet, daily.

Brach. Pander, ply your convoy, and leave your prating.

Flam. All your kindness to me, is like that miserable courtesy of Polyphemus to Ulysses; you reserve me to be devoured last: you would dig turfs out of my grave to feed your larks; that would be music to you. Come, I 'll lead you to her.

Brach. Do you face me?

Flam. Oh, sir, I would not go before a politic enemy with my back towards him, though there were behind me a whirlpool.

Enter Vittoria to Brachiano and Flamineo

Brach. Can you read, mistress? look upon that letter:
  There are no characters, nor hieroglyphics.
  You need no comment; I am grown your receiver.
  God's precious! you shall be a brave great lady,
  A stately and advanced whore.

Vit. Say, sir?

Brach. Come, come, let 's see your cabinet, discover
  Your treasury of love-letters. Death and furies!
  I 'll see them all.

Vit. Sir, upon my soul,
  I have not any. Whence was this directed?

61

Brach. Confusion on your politic ignorance!
  You are reclaim'd, are you? I 'll give you the bells,
  And let you fly to the devil.

Flam. Ware hawk, my lord.

Vit. Florence! this is some treacherous plot, my lord;
  To me he ne'er was lovely, I protest,
  So much as in my sleep.

Brach. Right! there are plots.
  Your beauty! Oh, ten thousand curses on 't!
  How long have I beheld the devil in crystal!
  Thou hast led me, like an heathen sacrifice,
  With music, and with fatal yokes of flowers,
  To my eternal ruin. Woman to man
  Is either a god, or a wolf.

Vit. My lord——

Brach. Away!
  We 'll be as differing as two adamants,
  The one shall shun the other. What! dost weep?
  Procure but ten of thy dissembling trade,
  Ye 'd furnish all the Irish funerals
  With howling past wild Irish.

Flam. Fie, my lord!

Brach. That hand, that cursed hand, which I have wearied
  With doting kisses!—Oh, my sweetest duchess,
  How lovely art thou now!—My loose thoughts
  Scatter like quicksilver: I was bewitch'd;
  For all the world speaks ill of thee.

Vit. No matter;
  I 'll live so now, I 'll make that world recant,
  And change her speeches. You did name your duchess.

Brach. Whose death God pardon!

Vit. Whose death God revenge
  On thee, most godless duke!

Flam. Now for two whirlwinds.

Vit. What have I gain'd by thee, but infamy?
  Thou hast stain'd the spotless honour of my house,
  And frighted thence noble society:
  Like those, which sick o' th' palsy, and retain
  Ill-scenting foxes 'bout them, are still shunn'd
  By those of choicer nostrils. What do you call this house?
  Is this your palace? did not the judge style it
  A house of penitent whores? who sent me to it?
  To this incontinent college? is 't not you?
  Is 't not your high preferment? go, go, brag
  How many ladies you have undone, like me.
  Fare you well, sir; let me hear no more of you!
  I had a limb corrupted to an ulcer,
  But I have cut it off; and now I 'll go
  Weeping to heaven on crutches. For your gifts,
  I will return them all, and I do wish
  That I could make you full executor
  To all my sins. O that I could toss myself
  Into a grave as quickly! for all thou art worth
  I 'll not shed one tear more—I 'll burst first.
                          [She throws herself upon a bed.

Brach. I have drunk Lethe: Vittoria!
  My dearest happiness! Vittoria!
  What do you ail, my love? why do you weep?

Vit. Yes, I now weep poniards, do you see?

Brach. Are not those matchless eyes mine?

Vit. I had rather
  They were not matches.

Brach. Is not this lip mine?

Vit. Yes; thus to bite it off, rather than give it thee.

Flam. Turn to my lord, good sister.

Vit. Hence, you pander!

Flam. Pander! am I the author of your sin?

Vit. Yes; he 's a base thief that a thief lets in.

Flam. We 're blown up, my lord——

Brach. Wilt thou hear me?
  Once to be jealous of thee, is t' express
  That I will love thee everlastingly,
  And never more be jealous.

Vit. O thou fool,
  Whose greatness hath by much o'ergrown thy wit!
  What dar'st thou do, that I not dare to suffer,
  Excepting to be still thy whore? for that,
  In the sea's bottom sooner thou shalt make
  A bonfire.

Flam. Oh, no oaths, for God's sake!

Brach. Will you hear me?

Vit. Never.

Flam. What a damn'd imposthume is a woman's will!
  Can nothing break it? [Aside.] Fie, fie, my lord,
  Women are caught as you take tortoises,
  She must be turn'd on her back. Sister, by this hand
  I am on your side.—Come, come, you have wrong'd her;
  What a strange credulous man were you, my lord,
  To think the Duke of Florenc would love her!
  Will any mercer take another's ware
  When once 'tis tows'd and sullied? And yet, sister,
  How scurvily this forwardness becomes you!
  Young leverets stand not long, and women's anger
  Should, like their flight, procure a little sport;
  A full cry for a quarter of an hour,
  And then be put to th' dead quat.

Brach. Shall these eyes,
  Which have so long time dwelt upon your face,
  Be now put out?

Flam. No cruel landlady i' th' world,
  Which lends forth groats to broom-men, and takes use
  For them, would do 't.
  Hand her, my lord, and kiss her: be not like
  A ferret, to let go your hold with blowing.

Brach. Let us renew right hands.

Vit. Hence!

Brach. Never shall rage, or the forgetful wine,
  Make me commit like fault.

Flam. Now you are i' th' way on 't, follow 't hard.

Brach. Be thou at peace with me, let all the world
  Threaten the cannon.

Flam. Mark his penitence;
  Best natures do commit the grossest faults,
  When they 're given o'er to jealousy, as best wine,
  Dying, makes strongest vinegar. I 'll tell you:
  The sea 's more rough and raging than calm rivers,
  But not so sweet, nor wholesome. A quiet woman
  Is a still water under a great bridge;
  A man may shoot her safely.

Vit. O ye dissembling men!

Flam. We suck'd that, sister,
  From women's breasts, in our first infancy.

Vit. To add misery to misery!

Brach. Sweetest!

Vit. Am I not low enough?
  Ay, ay, your good heart gathers like a snowball,
  Now your affection 's cold.

Flam. Ud's foot, it shall melt
  To a heart again, or all the wine in Rome
  Shall run o' th' lees for 't.

Vit. Your dog or hawk should be rewarded better
  Than I have been. I 'll speak not one word more.

Flam. Stop her mouth
  With a sweet kiss, my lord. So,
  Now the tide 's turn'd, the vessel 's come about.
  He 's a sweet armful. Oh, we curl-hair'd men
  Are still most kind to women! This is well.

Brach. That you should chide thus!

Flam. Oh, sir, your little chimneys
  Do ever cast most smoke! I sweat for you.
  Couple together with as deep a silence,
  As did the Grecians in their wooden horse.
  My lord, supply your promises with deeds;
  You know that painted meat no hunger feeds.

Brach. Stay, ungrateful Rome——

Flam. Rome! it deserve to be call'd Barbary,
  For our villainous usage.

Brach. Soft; the same project which the Duke of Florence,
  (Whether in love or gallery I know not)
  Laid down for her escape, will I pursue.

Flam. And no time fitter than this night, my lord.
  The Pope being dead, and all the cardinals enter'd
  The conclave, for th' electing a new Pope;
  The city in a great confusion;
  We may attire her in a page's suit,
  Lay her post-horse, take shipping, and amain
  For Padua.

Brach. I 'll instantly steal forth the Prince Giovanni,
  And make for Padua. You two with your old mother,
  And young Marcello that attends on Florence,
  If you can work him to it, follow me:
  I will advance you all; for you, Vittoria,
  Think of a duchess' title.

Flam. Lo you, sister!
  Stay, my lord; I 'll tell you a tale. The crocodile, which lives
  in the River Nilus, hath a worm breeds i' th' teeth of 't, which puts
  it to extreme anguish: a little bird, no bigger than a wren, is
  barber-surgeon to this crocodile; flies into the jaws of 't, picks out
  the worm, and brings present remedy. The fish, glad of ease, but
  ungrateful to her that did it, that the bird may not talk largely of
  her abroad for non-payment, closeth her chaps, intending to swallow
  her, and so put her to perpetual silence. But nature, loathing such
  ingratitude, hath armed this bird with a quill or prick on the head,
  top o' th' which wounds the crocodile i' th' mouth, forceth her open
  her bloody prison, and away flies the pretty tooth-picker from her
  cruel patient.

Brach. Your application is, I have not rewarded
  The service you have done me.

Flam. No, my lord.
  You, sister, are the crocodile: you are blemish'd in your fame, my lord
  cures it; and though the comparison hold not in every particle, yet
  observe, remember, what good the bird with the prick i' th' head hath
  done you, and scorn ingratitude.
  It may appear to some ridiculous
  Thus to talk knave and madman, and sometimes
  Come in with a dried sentence, stuffed with sage:
  But this allows my varying of shapes;
  Knaves do grow great by being great men's apes.

SCENE III

Enter Francisco, Lodovico, Gasparo, and six Ambassadors

Fran. So, my lord, I commend your diligence.
  Guard well the conclave; and, as the order is,
  Let none have conference with the cardinals.

Lodo. I shall, my lord. Room for the ambassadors.

Gas. They 're wondrous brave to-day: why do they wear
  These several habits?

Lodo. Oh, sir, they 're knights
  Of several orders:
  That lord i' th' black cloak, with the silver cross,
  Is Knight of Rhodes; the next, Knight of St. Michael;
  That, of the Golden Fleece; the Frenchman, there,
  Knight of the Holy Ghost; my Lord of Savoy,
  Knight of th' Annunciation; the Englishman
  Is Knight of th' honour'd Garter, dedicated
  Unto their saint, St. George. I could describe to you
  Their several institutions, with the laws
  Annexed to their orders; but that time
  Permits not such discovery.

Fran. Where 's Count Lodowick?

Lodo. Here, my lord.

Fran. 'Tis o' th' point of dinner time;
  Marshal the cardinals' service.

Lodo. Sir, I shall. [Enter Servants, with several dishes covered.
  Stand, let me search your dish. Who 's this for?

Servant. For my Lord Cardinal Monticelso.

Lodo. Whose this?

Servant. For my Lord Cardinal of Bourbon.

Fr. Ambass. Why doth he search the dishes? to observe
  What meat is dressed?

Eng. Ambass. No, sir, but to prevent
  Lest any letters should be convey'd in,
  To bribe or to solicit the advancement
  Of any cardinal. When first they enter,
  'Tis lawful for the ambassadors of princes
  To enter with them, and to make their suit
  For any man their prince affecteth best;
  But after, till a general election,
  No man may speak with them.

Lodo. You that attend on the lord cardinals,
  Open the window, and receive their viands.

Card. [Within.] You must return the service: the lord cardinals
  Are busied 'bout electing of the Pope;
  They have given o'er scrutiny, and are fallen
  To admiration.

Lodo. Away, away.

Fran. I 'll lay a thousand ducats you hear news
  Of a Pope presently. Hark; sure he 's elected:
  Behold, my Lord of Arragon appears
  On the church battlements. [A Cardinal on the terrace.

Arragon. Denuntio vobis gaudium magnum: Reverendissimus Cardinalis
  Lorenzo de Monticelso electus est in sedem apostolicam, et elegit sibi
  nomen Paulum Quartum.

Omnes. Vivat Sanctus Pater Paulus Quartus!

Servant. Vittoria, my lord——

Fran. Well, what of her?

Servant. Is fled the city——

Fran. Ha!

Servant. With Duke Brachiano.

Fran. Fled! where 's the Prince Giovanni?

Servant. Gone with his father.

Fran. Let the Matrona of the Convertites
  Be apprehended. Fled? O damnable!
  How fortunate are my wishes! why, 'twas this
  I only labour'd: I did send the letter
  T' instruct him what to do. Thy fame, fond duke,
  I first have poison'd; directed thee the way
  To marry a whore; what can be worse? This follows:
  The hand must act to drown the passionate tongue,
  I scorn to wear a sword and prate of wrong.

Enter Monticelso in State

Mont. Concedimus vobis Apostolicam benedictionem, et remissionem
  peccatorum.
  My lord reports Vittoria Corombona
  Is stol'n from forth the House of Convertites
  By Brachiano, and they 're fled the city.
  Now, though this be the first day of our seat,
  We cannot better please the Divine Power,
  Than to sequester from the Holy Church
  These cursed persons. Make it therefore known,
  We do denounce excommunication
  Against them both: all that are theirs in Rome
  We likewise banish. Set on.
                    [Exeunt all but Francisco and Lodovico.

Fran. Come, dear Lodovico;
  You have ta'en the sacrament to prosecute
  Th' intended murder?

Lodo. With all constancy.
  But, sir, I wonder you 'll engage yourself
  In person, being a great prince.

Fran. Divert me not.
  Most of his court are of my faction,
  And some are of my council. Noble friend,
  Our danger shall be like in this design:
  Give leave part of the glory may be mine. [Exit Francisco.

Enter Monticelso

Mont. Why did the Duke of Florence with such care
  Labour your pardon? say.

Lodo. Italian beggars will resolve you that,
  Who, begging of alms, bid those they beg of,
  Do good for their own sakes; or 't may be,
  He spreads his bounty with a sowing hand,
  Like kings, who many times give out of measure,
  Not for desert so much, as for their pleasure.

Mont. I know you 're cunning. Come, what devil was that
  That you were raising?

Lodo. Devil, my lord?

Mont. I ask you,
  How doth the duke employ you, that his bonnet
  Fell with such compliment unto his knee,
  When he departed from you?

Lodo. Why, my lord,
  He told me of a resty Barbary horse
  Which he would fain have brought to the career,
  The sault, and the ring galliard: now, my lord,
  I have a rare French rider.

Mont. Take your heed,
  Lest the jade break your neck. Do you put me off
  With your wild horse-tricks? Sirrah, you do lie.
  Oh, thou 'rt a foul black cloud, and thou dost threat
  A violent storm!

Lodo. Storms are i' th' air, my lord;
  I am too low to storm.

Mont. Wretched creature!
  I know that thou art fashion'd for all ill,
  Like dogs, that once get blood, they 'll ever kill.
  About some murder, was 't not?

Lodo. I 'll not tell you:
  And yet I care not greatly if I do;
  Marry, with this preparation. Holy father,
  I come not to you as an intelligencer,
  But as a penitent sinner: what I utter
  Is in confession merely; which, you know,
  Must never be reveal'd.

Mont. You have o'erta'en me.

Lodo. Sir, I did love Brachiano's duchess dearly,
  Or rather I pursued her with hot lust,
  Though she ne'er knew on 't. She was poison'd;
  Upon my soul she was: for which I have sworn
  T' avenge her murder.

Mont. To the Duke of Florence?

Lodo. To him I have.

Mont. Miserable creature!
  If thou persist in this, 'tis damnable.
  Dost thou imagine, thou canst slide on blood,
  And not be tainted with a shameful fall?
  Or, like the black and melancholic yew-tree,
  Dost think to root thyself in dead men's graves,
  And yet to prosper? Instruction to thee
  Comes like sweet showers to o'er-harden'd ground;
  They wet, but pierce not deep. And so I leave thee,
  With all the furies hanging 'bout thy neck,
  Till by thy penitence thou remove this evil,
  In conjuring from thy breast that cruel devil. [Exit.

Lodo. I 'll give it o'er; he says 'tis damnable:
  Besides I did expect his suffrage,
  By reason of Camillo's death.

Enter Servant and Francisco

Fran. Do you know that count?

Servant. Yes, my lord.

Fran. Bear him these thousand ducats to his lodging.
  Tell him the Pope hath sent them. Happily
  That will confirm more than all the rest. [Exit.

Servant. Sir.

Lodo. To me, sir?

Servant. His Holiness hath sent you a thousand crowns,
  And wills you, if you travel, to make him
  Your patron for intelligence.

Lodo. His creature ever to be commanded.—
  Why now 'tis come about. He rail'd upon me;
  And yet these crowns were told out, and laid ready,
  Before he knew my voyage. Oh, the art,
  The modest form of greatness! that do sit,
  Like brides at wedding-dinners, with their looks turn'd
  From the least wanton jests, their puling stomach
  Sick from the modesty, when their thoughts are loose,
  Even acting of those hot and lustful sports
  Are to ensue about midnight: such his cunning!
  He sounds my depth thus with a golden plummet.
  I am doubly arm'd now. Now to th' act of blood,
  There 's but three furies found in spacious hell,
  But in a great man's breast three thousand dwell. [Exit.

ACT V

SCENE I

A passage over the stage of Brachiano, Flamineo, Marcello, Hortensio,
  Corombona, Cornelia, Zanche, and others: Flamineo and Hortensio remain.

Flam. In all the weary minutes of my life,
  Day ne'er broke up till now. This marriage
  Confirms me happy.

Hort. 'Tis a good assurance.
  Saw you not yet the Moor that 's come to court?

Flam. Yes, and conferr'd with him i' th' duke's closet.
  I have not seen a goodlier personage,
  Nor ever talk'd with man better experience'd
  In State affairs, or rudiments of war.
  He hath, by report, serv'd the Venetian
  In Candy these twice seven years, and been chief
  In many a bold design.

Hort. What are those two
  That bear him company?

Flam. Two noblemen of Hungary, that, living in the emperor's service as commanders, eight years since, contrary to the expectation of the court entered into religion, in the strict Order of Capuchins; but, being not well settled in their undertaking, they left their Order, and returned to court; for which, being after troubled in conscience, they vowed their service against the enemies of Christ, went to Malta, were there knighted, and in their return back, at this great solemnity, they are resolved for ever to forsake the world, and settle themselves here in a house of Capuchins in Padua.

Hort. 'Tis strange.

Flam. One thing makes it so: they have vowed for ever to wear, next
  their bare bodies, those coats of mail they served in.

Hort. Hard penance!
  Is the Moor a Christian?

Flam. He is.

Hort. Why proffers he his service to our duke?

Flam. Because he understands there 's like to grow
  Some wars between us and the Duke of Florence,
  In which he hopes employment.
  I never saw one in a stern bold look
  Wear more command, nor in a lofty phrase
  Express more knowing, or more deep contempt
  Of our slight airy courtiers
  As if he travell'd all the princes' courts
  Of Christendom: in all things strives t' express,
  That all, that should dispute with him, may know,
  Glories, like glow-worms, afar off shine bright,
  But look'd to near, have neither heat nor light.
  The duke.

Enter Brachiano, Francisco disguised like Mulinassar, Lodovico
  and Gasparo, bearing their swords, their helmets down, Antonelli,
  Farnese.

Brach. You are nobly welcome. We have heard at full
  Your honourable service 'gainst the Turk.
  To you, brave Mulinassar, we assign
  A competent pension: and are inly sorry,
  The vows of those two worthy gentlemen
  Make them incapable of our proffer'd bounty.
  Your wish is, you may leave your warlike swords
  For monuments in our chapel: I accept it,
  As a great honour done me, and must crave
  Your leave to furnish out our duchess' revels.
  Only one thing, as the last vanity
  You e'er shall view, deny me not to stay
  To see a barriers prepar'd to-night:
  You shall have private standings. It hath pleas'd
  The great ambassadors of several princes,
  In their return from Rome to their own countries,
  To grace our marriage, and to honour me
  With such a kind of sport.

Fran. I shall persuade them to stay, my lord.

Brach. Set on there to the presence.
                    [Exeunt Brachiano, Flamineo, and Hortensio.

Lodo. Noble my lord, most fortunately welcome;
                    [The conspirators here embrace.

75

You have our vows, seal'd with the sacrament,
  To second your attempts.

Gas. And all things ready;
  He could not have invented his own ruin
  (Had he despair'd) with more propriety.

Lodo. You would not take my way.

Fran. 'Tis better order'd.

Lodo. T' have poison'd his prayer-book, or a pair of beads,
  The pummel of his saddle, his looking-glass,
  Or th' handle of his racket,—O, that, that!
  That while he had been bandying at tennis,
  He might have sworn himself to hell, and strook
  His soul into the hazard! Oh, my lord,
  I would have our plot be ingenious,
  And have it hereafter recorded for example,
  Rather than borrow example.

Fran. There 's no way
  More speeding that this thought on.

Lodo. On, then.

Fran. And yet methinks that this revenge is poor,
  Because it steals upon him like a thief:
  To have ta'en him by the casque in a pitch'd field,
  Led him to Florence——

Lodo. It had been rare: and there
  Have crown'd him with a wreath of stinking garlic,
  T' have shown the sharpness of his government,
  And rankness of his lust. Flamineo comes.
              [Exeunt Lodovico, Antonelli, and Gasparo.

Enter Flamineo, Marcello, and Zanche

Marc. Why doth this devil haunt you, say?

Flam. I know not:
  For by this light, I do not conjure for her.
  'Tis not so great a cunning as men think,
  To raise the devil; for here 's one up already;
  The greatest cunning were to lay him down.

76

Marc. She is your shame.

Flam. I pray thee pardon her.
  In faith, you see, women are like to burs,
  Where their affection throws them, there they 'll stick.

Zan. That is my countryman, a goodly person;
  When he 's at leisure, I 'll discourse with him
  In our own language.

Flam. I beseech you do. [Exit Zanche.
  How is 't, brave soldier? Oh, that I had seen
  Some of your iron days! I pray relate
  Some of your service to us.

Fran. 'Tis a ridiculous thing for a man to be his own chronicle: I did never wash my mouth
with mine own praise, for fear of getting a stinking breath.

Marc. You 're too stoical. The duke will expect other discourse from you.

Fran. I shall never flatter him: I have studied man too much to do that. What difference is
between the duke and I? no more than between two bricks, all made of one clay: only 't may
be one is placed in top of a turret, the other in the bottom of a well, by mere chance. If I were
placed as high as the duke, I should stick as fast, make as fair a show, and bear out weather
equally.

Flam. If this soldier had a patent to beg in churches, then he would tell them stories.

Marc. I have been a soldier too.

Fran. How have you thrived?

Marc. Faith, poorly.

Fran. That 's the misery of peace: only outsides are then respected. As ships seem very great
upon the river, which show very little upon the seas, so some men i' th' court seem
Colossuses in a chamber, who, if they came into the field, would appear pitiful pigmies.

Flam. Give me a fair room yet hung with arras, and some great cardinal to lug me by th' ears,
as his endeared minion.

Fran. And thou mayest do the devil knows what villainy.

Flam. And safely.

Fran. Right: you shall see in the country, in harvest-time, pigeons, though they destroy never so much corn, the farmer dare not present the fowling-piece to them: why? because they belong to the lord of the manor; whilst your poor sparrows, that belong to the Lord of Heaven, they go to the pot for 't.

Flam. I will now give you some politic instruction. The duke says he
 will give you pension; that 's but bare promise; get it under his hand.
 For I have known men that have come from serving against the Turk, for
 three or four months they have had pension to buy them new wooden legs,
 and fresh plasters; but after, 'twas not to be had. And this miserable
 courtesy shows as if a tormentor should give hot cordial drinks to one
 three-quarters dead o' th' rack, only to fetch the miserable soul again
 to endure more dog-days.
 [Exit Francisco. Enter Hortensio, a young Lord, Zanche, and two more.
 How now, gallants? what, are they ready for the barriers?

Young Lord. Yes: the lords are putting on their armour.

Hort. What 's he?

Flam. A new upstart; one that swears like a falconer, and will lie in the duke's ear day by day, like a maker of almanacs: and yet I knew him, since he came to th' court, smell worse of sweat than an under tennis-court keeper.

Hort. Look you, yonder 's your sweet mistress.

Flam. Thou art my sworn brother: I 'll tell thee, I do love that Moor, that witch, very constrainedly. She knows some of my villainy. I do love her just as a man holds a wolf by the ears; but for fear of her turning upon me, and pulling out my throat, I would let her go to the devil.

Hort. I hear she claims marriage of thee.

Flam. 'Faith, I made to her some such dark promise; and, in seeking to fly from 't, I run on, like a frighted dog with a bottle at 's tail, that fain would bite it off, and yet dares not look behind him. Now, my precious gipsy.

Zan. Ay, your love to me rather cools than heats.

Flam. Marry, I am the sounder lover; we have many wenches about the town heat too fast.

Hort. What do you think of these perfumed gallants, then?

Flam. Their satin cannot save them: I am confident
 They have a certain spice of the disease;
 For they that sleep with dogs shall rise with fleas.

Zan. Believe it, a little painting and gay clothes make you loathe me.

Flam. How, love a lady for painting or gay apparel? I 'll unkennel one example more for thee. Æsop had a foolish dog that let go the flesh to catch the shadow; I would have courtiers be better diners.

Zan. You remember your oaths?

Flam. Lovers' oaths are like mariners' prayers, uttered in extremity; but when the tempest is o'er, and that the vessel leaves tumbling, they fall from protesting to drinking. And yet, amongst gentlemen, protesting and drinking go together, and agree as well as shoemakers and Westphalia bacon: they are both drawers on; for drink draws on protestation, and protestation draws on more drink. Is not this discourse better now than the morality of your sunburnt gentleman?

Enter Cornelia

Corn. Is this your perch, you haggard? fly to th' stews.
      [Strikes Zanche.

Flam. You should be clapped by th' heels now: strike i' th' court!
      [Exit Cornelia.

Zan. She 's good for nothing, but to make her maids
 Catch cold a-nights: they dare not use a bedstaff,
 For fear of her light fingers.

Marc. You 're a strumpet,
 An impudent one. [Kicks Zanche.

Flam. Why do you kick her, say?
 Do you think that she 's like a walnut tree?
 Must she be cudgell'd ere she bear good fruit?

Marc. She brags that you shall marry her.

Flam. What then?

Marc. I had rather she were pitch'd upon a stake,
 In some new-seeded garden, to affright
 Her fellow crows thence.

Flam. You 're a boy, a fool,
 Be guardian to your hound; I am of age.

Marc. If I take her near you, I 'll cut her throat.

Flam. With a fan of feather?

Marc. And, for you, I 'll whip
  This folly from you.

Flam. Are you choleric?
  I 'll purge it with rhubarb.

Hort. Oh, your brother!

Flam. Hang him,
  He wrongs me most, that ought t' offend me least:
  I do suspect my mother play'd foul play,
  When she conceiv'd thee.

Marc. Now, by all my hopes,
  Like the two slaughter'd sons of dipus,
  The very flames of our affection
  Shall turn two ways. Those words I 'll make thee answer
  With thy heart-blood.

Flam. Do, like the geese in the progress;
  You know where you shall find me.

Marc. Very good. [Exit Flamineo.
  And thou be'st a noble friend, bear him my sword,
  And bid him fit the length on 't.

Young Lord. Sir, I shall. [Exeunt all but Zanche.

Zan. He comes. Hence petty thought of my disgrace!
                    [Enter Francisco.
  I ne'er lov'd my complexion till now,
  'Cause I may boldly say, without a blush,
  I love you.

Fran. Your love is untimely sown; there 's a spring at Michaelmas, but 'tis but a faint one: I am sunk in years, and I have vowed never to marry.

Zan. Alas! poor maids get more lovers than husbands: yet you may mistake my wealth. For, as when ambassadors are sent to congratulate princes, there 's commonly sent along with them a rich present, so that, though the prince like not the ambassador's person, nor words, yet he likes well of the presentment; so I may come to you in the same manner, and be better loved for my dowry than my virtue.

Fran. I 'll think on the motion.

Zan. Do; I 'll now detain you no longer. At your better leisure, I 'll
   tell you things shall startle your blood:
   Nor blame me that this passion I reveal;
   Lovers die inward that their flames conceal.

Fran. Of all intelligence this may prove the best:
   Sure I shall draw strange fowl from this foul nest. [Exeunt.

SCENE II

Enter Marcello and Cornelia

Corn. I hear a whispering all about the court,
  You are to fight: who is your opposite?
  What is the quarrel?

Marc. 'Tis an idle rumour.

Corn. Will you dissemble? sure you do not well
  To fright me thus: you never look thus pale,
  But when you are most angry. I do charge you,
  Upon my blessing—nay, I 'll call the duke,
  And he shall school you.

Marc. Publish not a fear,
  Which would convert to laughter: 'tis not so.
  Was not this crucifix my father's?

Corn. Yes.

Marc. I have heard you say, giving my brother suck
  He took the crucifix between his hands, [Enter Flamineo.
  And broke a limb off.

Corn. Yes, but 'tis mended.

Flam. I have brought your weapon back.
                  [Flamineo runs Marcello through.

Corn. Ha! Oh, my horror!

Marc. You have brought it home, indeed.

Corn. Help! Oh, he 's murder'd!

Flam. Do you turn your gall up? I 'll to sanctuary,
  And send a surgeon to you. [Exit.

Enter Lodovico, Hortensio, and Gasparo

Hort. How! o' th' ground!

Marc. Oh, mother, now remember what I told
  Of breaking of the crucifix! Farewell.
  There are some sins, which heaven doth duly punish

In a whole family. This it is to rise
By all dishonest means! Let all men know,
That tree shall long time keep a steady foot,
Whose branches spread no wider than the root. [Dies.

Corn. Oh, my perpetual sorrow!

Hort. Virtuous Marcello!
 He 's dead. Pray leave him, lady: come, you shall.

Corn. Alas! he is not dead; he 's in a trance. Why, here 's nobody shall get anything by his death. Let me call him again, for God's sake!

Lodo. I would you were deceived.

Corn. Oh, you abuse me, you abuse me, you abuse me! how many have gone away thus, for lack of 'tendance! rear up 's head, rear up 's head! his bleeding inward will kill him.

Hort. You see he is departed.

Corn. Let me come to him; give me him as he is, if he be turn'd to earth; let me but give him one hearty kiss, and you shall put us both in one coffin. Fetch a looking-glass: see if his breath will not stain it; or pull out some feathers from my pillow, and lay them to his lips. Will you lose him for a little painstaking?

Hort. Your kindest office is to pray for him.

Corn. Alas! I would not pray for him yet. He may live to lay me i' th' ground, and pray for me, if you 'll let me come to him.

Enter Brachiano, all armed, save the beaver, with Flamineo and others

Brach. Was this your handiwork?

Flam. It was my misfortune.

Corn. He lies, he lies! he did not kill him: these have killed him, that would not let him be better looked to.

Brach. Have comfort, my griev'd mother.

Corn. Oh, you screech-owl!

Hort. Forbear, good madam.

Corn. Let me go, let me go.
[She runs to Flamineo with her knife drawn, and coming to him lets it
fall.
The God of heaven forgive thee! Dost not wonder
I pray for thee? I 'll tell thee what 's the reason,
I have scarce breath to number twenty minutes;
I 'd not spend that in cursing. Fare thee well:
Half of thyself lies there; and mayst thou live
To fill an hour-glass with his moulder'd ashes,
To tell how thou shouldst spend the time to come
In blessed repentance!

Brach. Mother, pray tell me
How came he by his death? what was the quarrel?

Corn. Indeed, my younger boy presum'd too much
Upon his manhood, gave him bitter words,
Drew his sword first; and so, I know not how,
For I was out of my wits, he fell with 's head
Just in my bosom.

Page. That is not true, madam.

Corn. I pray thee, peace.
One arrow 's graze'd already; it were vain
T' lose this, for that will ne'er be found again.

Brach. Go, bear the body to Cornelia's lodging:
And we command that none acquaint our duchess
With this sad accident. For you, Flamineo,
Hark you, I will not grant your pardon.

Flam. No?

Brach. Only a lease of your life; and that shall last
But for one day: thou shalt be forc'd each evening
To renew it, or be hang'd.

Flam. At your pleasure.
[Lodovico sprinkles Brachiano's beaver with a poison.
Enter Francisco
Your will is law now, I 'll not meddle with it.

Brach. You once did brave me in your sister's lodging:
I 'll now keep you in awe for 't. Where 's our beaver?

84

Fran. [Aside.] He calls for his destruction. Noble youth,
I pity thy sad fate! Now to the barriers.
This shall his passage to the black lake further;
The last good deed he did, he pardon'd murder. [Exeunt.

SCENE III

Charges and shouts. They fight at barriers; first single pairs, then three to three

Enter Brachiano and Flamineo, with others

Brach. An armourer! ud's death, an armourer!

Flam. Armourer! where 's the armourer?

Brach. Tear off my beaver.

Flam. Are you hurt, my lord?

Brach. Oh, my brain 's on fire! [Enter Armourer.
  The helmet is poison'd.

Armourer. My lord, upon my soul——

Brach. Away with him to torture.
  There are some great ones that have hand in this,
  And near about me.

Enter Vittoria Corombona

Vit. Oh, my lov'd lord! poison'd!

Flam. Remove the bar. Here 's unfortunate revels!
  Call the physicians. [Enter two Physicians.
  A plague upon you!
  We have too much of your cunning here already:
  I fear the ambassadors are likewise poison'd.

Brach. Oh, I am gone already! the infection
  Flies to the brain and heart. O thou strong heart!
  There 's such a covenant 'tween the world and it,
  They 're loath to break.

Giov. Oh, my most loved father!

Brach. Remove the boy away.
  Where 's this good woman? Had I infinite worlds,
  They were too little for thee: must I leave thee?
  What say you, screech-owls, is the venom mortal?

Physicians. Most deadly.

Brach. Most corrupted politic hangman,
 You kill without book; but your art to save
 Fails you as oft as great men's needy friends.
 I that have given life to offending slaves,
 And wretched murderers, have I not power
 To lengthen mine own a twelvemonth?
 [To Vittoria.] Do not kiss me, for I shall poison thee.
 This unctions 's sent from the great Duke of Florence.

Fran. Sir, be of comfort.

Brach. O thou soft natural death, that art joint-twin
 To sweetest slumber! no rough-bearded comet
 Stares on thy mild departure; the dull owl
 Bears not against thy casement; the hoarse wolf
 Scents not thy carrion: pity winds thy corse,
 Whilst horror waits on princes'.

Vit. I am lost for ever.

Brach. How miserable a thing it is to die
 'Mongst women howling! [Enter Lodovico and Gasparo, as Capuchins.
 What are those?

Flam. Franciscans:
 They have brought the extreme unction.

Brach. On pain of death, let no man name death to me:
 It is a word infinitely terrible.
 Withdraw into our cabinet.
                [Exeunt all but Francisco and Flamineo.

Flam. To see what solitariness is about dying princes! as heretofore they have unpeopled towns, divorced friends, and made great houses unhospitable, so now, O justice! where are their flatterers now? flatterers are but the shadows of princes' bodies; the least thick cloud makes them invisible.

Fran. There 's great moan made for him.

Flam. 'Faith, for some few hours salt-water will run most plentifully in every office o' th' court; but, believe it, most of them do weep over their stepmothers' graves.

Fran. How mean you?

Flam. Why, they dissemble; as some men do that live without compass o' th' verge.

87

Fran. Come, you have thrived well under him.

Flam. 'Faith, like a wolf in a woman's breast; I have been fed with poultry: but for money, understand me, I had as good a will to cozen him as e'er an officer of them all; but I had not cunning enough to do it.

Fran. What didst thou think of him? 'faith, speak freely.

Flam. He was a kind of statesman, that would sooner have reckoned how many cannon-bullets he had discharged against a town, to count his expense that way, than think how many of his valiant and deserving subjects he lost before it.

Fran. Oh, speak well of the duke!

Flam. I have done. [Enter Lodovico. Wilt hear some of my court-wisdom? To reprehend princes is dangerous; and to over-commend some of them is palpable lying.

Fran. How is it with the duke?

Lodo. Most deadly ill.
  He 's fallen into a strange distraction:
  He talks of battles and monopolies,
  Levying of taxes; and from that descends
  To the most brain-sick language. His mind fastens
  On twenty several objects, which confound
  Deep sense with folly. Such a fearful end
  May teach some men that bear too lofty crest,
  Though they live happiest yet they die not best.
  He hath conferr'd the whole state of the dukedom
  Upon your sister, till the prince arrive
  At mature age.

Flam. There 's some good luck in that yet.

Fran. See, here he comes.
        [Enter Brachiano, presented in a bed, Vittoria and others.
  There 's death in 's face already.

Vit. Oh, my good lord!

Brach. Away, you have abus'd me:
    [These speeches are several kinds of distractions, and in the action
      should appear so.
  You have convey'd coin forth our territories,
  Bought and sold offices, oppress'd the poor,

88

And I ne'er dreamt on 't. Make up your accounts,
  I 'll now be mine own steward.

Flam. Sir, have patience.

Brach. Indeed, I am to blame:
  For did you ever hear the dusky raven
  Chide blackness? or was 't ever known the devil
  Rail'd against cloven creatures?

Vit. Oh, my lord!

Brach. Let me have some quails to supper.

Flam. Sir, you shall.

Brach. No, some fried dog-fish; your quails feed on poison.
  That old dog-fox, that politician, Florence!
  I 'll forswear hunting, and turn dog-killer.
  Rare! I 'll be friends with him; for, mark you, sir, one dog
  Still sets another a-barking. Peace, peace!
  Yonder 's a fine slave come in now.

Flam. Where?

Brach. Why, there,
  In a blue bonnet, and a pair of breeches
  With a great cod-piece: ha, ha, ha!
  Look you, his cod-piece is stuck full of pins,
  With pearls o' th' head of them. Do you not know him?

Flam. No, my lord.

Brach. Why, 'tis the devil.
  I know him by a great rose he wears on 's shoe,
  To hide his cloven foot. I 'll dispute with him;
  He 's a rare linguist.

Vit. My lord, here 's nothing.

Brach. Nothing! rare! nothing! when I want money,
  Our treasury is empty, there is nothing:
  I 'll not be use'd thus.

Vit. Oh, lie still, my lord!

Brach. See, see Flamineo, that kill'd his brother,
  Is dancing on the ropes there, and he carries
  A money-bag in each hand, to keep him even,
  For fear of breaking 's neck: and there 's a lawyer,
  In a gown whipped with velvet, stares and gapes
  When the money will fall. How the rogue cuts capers!
  It should have been in a halter. 'Tis there; what 's she?

Flam. Vittoria, my lord.

Brach. Ha, ha, ha! her hair is sprinkl'd with orris powder,
  That makes her look as if she had sinn'd in the pastry.
  What 's he?

Flam. A divine, my lord.
  [Brachiano seems here near his end; Lodovico and Gasparo, in the habit
    of Capuchins, present him in his bed with a crucifix and hallowed
    candle.

Brach. He will be drunk; avoid him: th' argument
  Is fearful, when churchmen stagger in 't.
  Look you, six grey rats that have lost their tails
  Crawl upon the pillow; send for a rat-catcher:
  I 'll do a miracle, I 'll free the court
  From all foul vermin. Where 's Flamineo?

Flam. I do not like that he names me so often,
  Especially on 's death-bed; 'tis a sign
  I shall not live long. See, he 's near his end.

Lodo. Pray, give us leave. Attende, domine Brachiane.

Flam. See how firmly he doth fix his eye
  Upon the crucifix.

Vit. Oh, hold it constant!
  It settles his wild spirits; and so his eyes
  Melt into tears.

Lodo. Domine Brachiane, solebas in bello tutus esse tuo clypeo; nunc
  hunc clypeum hosti tuo opponas infernali. [By the crucifix.

Gas. Olim hastâ valuisti in bello; nunc hanc sacram hastam vibrabis
  contra hostem animarum. [By the hallowed taper.

90

Lodo. Attende, Domine Brachiane, si nunc quoque probes ea, quæ acta
  sunt inter nos, flecte caput in dextrum.

Gas. Esto securus, Domine Brachiane; cogita, quantum habeas meritorum;
  denique memineris mean animam pro tuâ oppignoratum si quid esset
  periculi.

Lodo. Si nunc quoque probas ea, quæ acta sunt inter nos, flecte caput
  in lvum.
  He is departing: pray stand all apart,
  And let us only whisper in his ears
  Some private meditations, which our order
  Permits you not to hear.
[Here, the rest being departed, Lodovico and Gasparo discover themselves.

Gas. Brachiano.

Lodo. Devil Brachiano, thou art damn'd.

Gas. Perpetually.

Lodo. A slave condemn'd and given up to the gallows,
  Is thy great lord and master.

Gas. True; for thou
  Art given up to the devil.

Lodo. Oh, you slave!
  You that were held the famous politician,
  Whose art was poison.

Gas. And whose conscience, murder.

Lodo. That would have broke your wife's neck down the stairs,
  Ere she was poison'd.

Gas. That had your villainous sallets.

Lodo. And fine embroider'd bottles, and perfumes,
  Equally mortal with a winter plague.

Gas. Now there 's mercury——

Lodo. And copperas——

Gas. And quicksilver——

Lodo. With other devilish 'pothecary stuff,
  A-melting in your politic brains: dost hear?

Gas. This is Count Lodovico.

Lodo. This, Gasparo:
  And thou shalt die like a poor rogue.

Gas. And stink
  Like a dead fly-blown dog.

Lodo. And be forgotten
  Before the funeral sermon.

Brach. Vittoria! Vittoria!

Lodo. Oh, the cursed devil
  Comes to himself a gain! we are undone.

Gas. Strangle him in private. [Enter Vittoria and the Attendants.
  What? Will you call him again to live in treble torments?
  For charity, for christian charity, avoid the chamber.

Lodo. You would prate, sir? This is a true-love knot
  Sent from the Duke of Florence. [Brachiano is strangled.

Gas. What, is it done?

Lodo. The snuff is out. No woman-keeper i' th' world,
  Though she had practis'd seven year at the pest-house,
  Could have done 't quaintlier. My lords, he 's dead.

Vittoria and the others come forward

Omnes. Rest to his soul!

Vit. Oh me! this place is hell.

Fran. How heavily she takes it!

Flam. Oh, yes, yes;
  Had women navigable rivers in their eyes,
  They would dispend them all. Surely, I wonder
  Why we should wish more rivers to the city,
  When they sell water so good cheap. I 'll tell thee
  These are but Moorish shades of griefs or fears;

92

There 's nothing sooner dry than women's tears.
Why, here 's an end of all my harvest; he has given me nothing.
Court promises! let wise men count them curs'd;
For while you live, he that scores best, pays worst.

Fran. Sure this was Florence' doing.

Flam. Very likely:
  Those are found weighty strokes which come from th' hand,
  But those are killing strokes which come from th' head.
  Oh, the rare tricks of a Machiavellian!
  He doth not come, like a gross plodding slave,
  And buffet you to death; no, my quaint knave,
  He tickles you to death, makes you die laughing,
  As if you had swallow'd down a pound of saffron.
  You see the feat, 'tis practis'd in a trice;
  To teach court honesty, it jumps on ice.

Fran. Now have the people liberty to talk,
  And descant on his vices.

Flam. Misery of princes,
  That must of force be censur'd by their slaves!
  Not only blam'd for doing things are ill,
  But for not doing all that all men will:
  One were better be a thresher.
  Ud's death! I would fain speak with this duke yet.

Fran. Now he 's dead?

Flam. I cannot conjure; but if prayers or oaths
  Will get to th' speech of him, though forty devils
  Wait on him in his livery of flames,
  I 'll speak to him, and shake him by the hand,
  Though I be blasted. [Exit.

Fran. Excellent Lodovico!
  What! did you terrify him at the last gasp?

Lodo. Yes, and so idly, that the duke had like
  T' have terrified us.

Fran. How?

Enter the Moor

93

Lodo. You shall hear that hereafter.
  See, yon 's the infernal, that would make up sport.
  Now to the revelation of that secret
  She promis'd when she fell in love with you.

Fran. You 're passionately met in this sad world.

Zan. I would have you look up, sir; these court tears
  Claim not your tribute to them: let those weep,
  That guiltily partake in the sad cause.
  I knew last night, by a sad dream I had,
  Some mischief would ensue: yet, to say truth,
  My dream most concern'd you.

Lodo. Shall 's fall a-dreaming?

Fran. Yes, and for fashion sake I 'll dream with her.

Zan. Methought, sir, you came stealing to my bed.

Fran. Wilt thou believe me, sweeting? by this light
  I was a-dreamt on thee too; for methought
  I saw thee naked.

Zan. Fie, sir! as I told you,
  Methought you lay down by me.

Fran. So dreamt I;
  And lest thou shouldst take cold, I cover'd thee
  With this Irish mantle.

Zan. Verily I did dream
  You were somewhat bold with me: but to come to 't——

Lodo. How! how! I hope you will not got to 't here.

Fran. Nay, you must hear my dream out.

Zan. Well, sir, forth.

Fran. When I threw the mantle o'er thee, thou didst laugh
  Exceedingly, methought.

Zan. Laugh!

Fran. And criedst out, the hair did tickle thee.

Zan. There was a dream indeed!

Lodo. Mark her, I pray thee, she simpers like the suds
  A collier hath been wash'd in.

Zan. Come, sir; good fortune tends you. I did tell you
  I would reveal a secret: Isabella,
  The Duke of Florence' sister, was empoisone'd
  By a fum'd picture; and Camillo's neck
  Was broke by damn'd Flamineo, the mischance
  Laid on a vaulting-horse.

Fran. Most strange!

Zan. Most true.

Lodo. The bed of snakes is broke.

Zan. I sadly do confess, I had a hand
  In the black deed.

Fran. Thou kept'st their counsel.

Zan. Right;
  For which, urg'd with contrition, I intend
  This night to rob Vittoria.

Lodo. Excellent penitence!
  Usurers dream on 't while they sleep out sermons.

Zan. To further our escape, I have entreated
  Leave to retire me, till the funeral,
  Unto a friend i' th' country: that excuse
  Will further our escape. In coin and jewels
  I shall at least make good unto your use
  An hundred thousand crowns.

Fran. Oh, noble wench!

Lodo. Those crowns we 'll share.

Zan. It is a dowry,
  Methinks, should make that sun-burnt proverb false,
  And wash the Æthiop white.

Fran. It shall; away.

Zan. Be ready for our flight.

Fran. An hour 'fore day. [Exit Zanche.
  Oh, strange discovery! why, till now we knew not
  The circumstances of either of their deaths.

Re-enter Zanche

Zan. You 'll wait about midnight in the chapel?

Fran. There. [Exit Zanche.

Lodo. Why, now our action 's justified.

Fran. Tush for justice!
  What harms it justice? we now, like the partridge,
  Purge the disease with laurel; for the fame
  Shall crown the enterprise, and quit the shame. [Exeunt.

SCENE IV

Enter Flamineo and Gasparo, at one door; another way, Giovanni, attended

Gas. The young duke: did you e'er see a sweeter prince?

Flam. I have known a poor woman's bastard better favoured—this is behind him. Now, to his face—all comparisons were hateful. Wise was the courtly peacock, that, being a great minion, and being compared for beauty by some dottrels that stood by to the kingly eagle, said the eagle was a far fairer bird than herself, not in respect of her feathers, but in respect of her long talons: his will grow out in time. —My gracious lord.

Giov. I pray leave me, sir.

Flam. Your grace must be merry; 'tis I have cause to mourn; for wot you, what said the little boy that rode behind his father on horseback?

Giov. Why, what said he?

Flam. When you are dead, father, said he, I hope that I shall ride in the saddle. Oh, 'tis a brave thing for a man to sit by himself! he may stretch himself in the stirrups, look about, and see the whole compass of the hemisphere. You 're now, my lord, i' th' saddle.

Giov. Study your prayers, sir, and be penitent:
  'Twere fit you 'd think on what hath former been;
  I have heard grief nam'd the eldest child of sin. [Exit.

Flam. Study my prayers! he threatens me divinely! I am falling to
  pieces already. I care not, though, like Anacharsis, I were pounded to
  death in a mortar: and yet that death were fitter for usurers, gold and
  themselves to be beaten together, to make a most cordial cullis for the
  devil.
  He hath his uncle's villainous look already,
  In decimo-sexto. [Enter Courtier.] Now, sir, what are you?

Court. It is the pleasure, sir, of the young duke,
  That you forbear the presence, and all rooms
  That owe him reverence.

Flam. So the wolf and the raven are very pretty fools when they are
  young. It is your office, sir, to keep me out?

Court. So the duke wills.

Flam. Verily, Master Courtier, extremity is not to be used in all offices: say, that a gentlewoman were taken out of her bed about midnight, and committed to Castle Angelo, to the tower yonder, with nothing about her but her smock, would it not show a cruel part in the gentleman-porter to lay claim to her upper garment, pull it o'er her head and ears, and put her in naked?

Court. Very good: you are merry. [Exit.

Flam. Doth he make a court-ejectment of me? a flaming fire-brand casts
  more smoke without a chimney than within 't.
  I 'll smoor some of them. [Enter Francisco de Medicis.
  How now? thou art sad.

Fran. I met even now with the most piteous sight.

Flam. Thou meet'st another here, a pitiful
  Degraded courtier.

Fran. Your reverend mother
  Is grown a very old woman in two hours.
  I found them winding of Marcello's corse;
  And there is such a solemn melody,
  'Tween doleful songs, tears, and sad elegies;
  Such as old granddames, watching by the dead,
  Were wont t' outwear the nights with that, believe me,
  I had no eyes to guide me forth the room,
  They were so o'ercharg'd with water.

Flam. I will see them.

Fran. 'Twere much uncharity in you; for your sight
  Will add unto their tears.

Flam. I will see them:
  They are behind the traverse; I 'll discover
  Their superstitions howling.
    [He draws the traverse. Cornelia, the Moor, and three other
      Ladies discovered winding Marcello's corse. A song.

Corn. This rosemary is wither'd; pray, get fresh.
  I would have these herbs grow upon his grave,
  When I am dead and rotten. Reach the bays,
  I 'll tie a garland here about his head;
  I have kept this twenty year, and every day
  Hallow'd it with my prayers; I did not think
  He should have wore it.

Zan. Look you, who are yonder?

Corn. Oh, reach me the flowers!

Zan. Her ladyship 's foolish.

Woman. Alas, her grief
  Hath turn'd her child again!

Corn. You 're very welcome: [To Flamineo.
  There 's rosemary for you, and rue for you,
  Heart's-ease for you; I pray make much of it,
  I have left more for myself.

Fran. Lady, who 's this?

Corn. You are, I take it, the grave-maker.

Flam. So.

Zan. 'Tis Flamineo.

Corn. Will you make me such a fool? here 's a white hand:
  Can blood so soon be washed out? let me see;
  When screech-owls croak upon the chimney-tops,
  And the strange cricket i' th' oven sings and hops,
  When yellow spots do on your hands appear,
  Be certain then you of a corse shall hear.
  Out upon 't, how 'tis speckled! h' 'as handled a toad sure.
  Cowslip water is good for the memory:
  Pray, buy me three ounces of 't.

Flam. I would I were from hence.

Corn. Do you hear, sir?
  I 'll give you a saying which my grandmother
  Was wont, when she heard the bell toll, to sing o'er
  Unto her lute.

Flam. Do, an you will, do.

Corn. Call for the robin redbreast, and the wren,
          [Cornelia doth this in several forms of distraction.
  Since o'er shady groves they hover,
  And with leaves and flowers do cover
  The friendless bodies of unburied men.

Call unto his funeral dole
The ant, the fieldmouse, and the mole,
To rear him hillocks that shall keep him warm,
And (when gay tombs are robb'd) sustain no harm;
But keep the wolf far thence, that 's foe to men,
For with his nails he 'll dig them up again.
They would not bury him 'cause he died in a quarrel;
But I have an answer for them:
Let holy Church receive him duly,
Since he paid the church-tithes truly.
His wealth is summ'd, and this is all his store,
This poor men get, and great men get no more.
Now the wares are gone, we may shut up shop.
Bless you all, good people. [Exeunt Cornelia and Ladies.

Flam. I have a strange thing in me, to th' which
  I cannot give a name, without it be
  Compassion. I pray leave me. [Exit Francisco.
  This night I 'll know the utmost of my fate;
  I 'll be resolv'd what my rich sister means
  T' assign me for my service. I have liv'd
  Riotously ill, like some that live in court,
  And sometimes when my face was full of smiles,
  Have felt the maze of conscience in my breast.
  Oft gay and honour'd robes those tortures try:
  We think cag'd birds sing, when indeed they cry.

Enter Brachiano's Ghost, in his leather cassock and breeches, boots, a
  cowl, a pot of lily flowers, with a skull in 't

  Ha! I can stand thee: nearer, nearer yet.
  What a mockery hath death made thee! thou look'st sad.
  In what place art thou? in yon starry gallery?
  Or in the cursed dungeon? No? not speak?
  Pray, sir, resolve me, what religion 's best
  For a man to die in? or is it in your knowledge
  To answer me how long I have to live?
  That 's the most necessary question.
  Not answer? are you still, like some great men
  That only walk like shadows up and down,
  And to no purpose; say——
        [The Ghost throws earth upon him, and shows him the skull.
  What 's that? O fatal! he throws earth upon me.
  A dead man's skull beneath the roots of flowers!

100

I pray speak, sir: our Italian churchmen
Make us believe dead men hold conference
With their familiars, and many times
Will come to bed with them, and eat with them. [Exit Ghost.
He 's gone; and see, the skull and earth are vanish'd.
This is beyond melancholy. I do dare my fate
To do its worst. Now to my sister's lodging,
And sum up all those horrors: the disgrace
The prince threw on me; next the piteous sight
Of my dead brother; and my mother's dotage;
And last this terrible vision: all these
Shall with Vittoria's bounty turn to good,
Or I will drown this weapon in her blood. [Exit.

SCENE V

Enter Francisco, Lodovico, and Hortensio

Lodo. My lord, upon my soul you shall no further;
  You have most ridiculously engag'd yourself
  To far already. For my part, I have paid
  All my debts: so, if I should chance to fall,
  My creditors fall not with me; and I vow,
  To quit all in this bold assembly,
  To the meanest follower. My lord, leave the city,
  Or I 'll forswear the murder. [Exit.

Fran. Farewell, Lodovico:
  If thou dost perish in this glorious act,
  I 'll rear unto thy memory that fame,
  Shall in the ashes keep alive thy name. [Exit.

Hort. There 's some black deed on foot. I 'll presently
  Down to the citadel, and raise some force.
  These strong court-factions, that do brook no checks,
  In the career oft break the riders' necks. [Exit.

SCENE VI

Enter Vittoria with a book in her hand, Zanche; Flamineo following them

Flam. What, are you at your prayers? Give o'er.

Vit. How, ruffian?

Flam. I come to you 'bout worldly business.
  Sit down, sit down. Nay, stay, blowze, you may hear it:
  The doors are fast enough.

Vit. Ha! are you drunk?

Flam. Yes, yes, with wormwood water; you shall taste
  Some of it presently.

Vit. What intends the fury?

Flam. You are my lord's executrix; and I claim
  Reward for my long service.

Vit. For your service!

Flam. Come, therefore, here is pen and ink, set down
  What you will give me.

Vit. There. [She writes.

Flam. Ha! have you done already?
  'Tis a most short conveyance.

Vit. I will read it:
  I give that portion to thee, and no other,
  Which Cain groan'd under, having slain his brother.

Flam. A most courtly patent to beg by.

Vit. You are a villain!

Flam. Is 't come to this? they say affrights cure agues:
  Thou hast a devil in thee; I will try
  If I can scare him from thee. Nay, sit still:
  My lord hath left me yet two cases of jewels,
  Shall make me scorn your bounty; you shall see them. [Exit.

Vit. Sure he 's distracted.

Zan. Oh, he 's desperate!
  For your own safety give him gentle language.
                    [He enters with two cases of pistols.

Flam. Look, these are better far at a dead lift,
  Than all your jewel house.

Vit. And yet, methinks,
  These stones have no fair lustre, they are ill set.

Flam. I 'll turn the right side towards you: you shall see
  How they will sparkle.

Vit. Turn this horror from me!
  What do you want? what would you have me do?
  Is not all mine yours? have I any children?

Flam. Pray thee, good woman, do not trouble me
  With this vain worldly business; say your prayers:
  Neither yourself nor I should outlive him
  The numbering of four hours.

Vit. Did he enjoin it?

Flam. He did, and 'twas a deadly jealousy,
  Lest any should enjoy thee after him,
  That urged him vow me to it. For my death,
  I did propound it voluntarily, knowing,
  If he could not be safe in his own court,
  Being a great duke, what hope then for us?

Vit. This is your melancholy, and despair.

Flam. Away:
  Fool thou art, to think that politicians
  DO use to kill the effects or injuries
  And let the cause live. Shall we groan in irons,
  Or be a shameful and a weighty burthen
  To a public scaffold? This is my resolve:
  I would not live at any man's entreaty,
  Nor die at any's bidding.

Vit. Will you hear me?

Flam. My life hath done service to other men,
  My death shall serve mine own turn: make you ready.

Vit. Do you mean to die indeed?

Flam. With as much pleasure,
  As e'er my father gat me.

Vit. Are the doors lock'd?

Zan. Yes, madam.

Vit. Are you grown an atheist? will you turn your body,
  Which is the goodly palace of the soul,
  To the soul's slaughter-house? Oh, the cursed devil,
  Which doth present us with all other sins
  Thrice candied o'er, despair with gall and stibium;
  Yet we carouse it off. [Aside to Zanche.] Cry out for help!
  Makes us forsake that which was made for man,
  The world, to sink to that was made for devils,
  Eternal darkness!

Zan. Help, help!

Flam. I 'll stop your throat
  With winter plums.

Vit. I pray thee yet remember,
  Millions are now in graves, which at last day
  Like mandrakes shall rise shrieking.

Flam. Leave your prating,
  For these are but grammatical laments,
  Feminine arguments: and they move me,
  As some in pulpits move their auditory,
  More with their exclamation than sense
  Of reason, or sound doctrine.

Zan. [Aside.] Gentle madam,
  Seem to consent, only persuade him to teach
  The way to death; let him die first.

Vit. 'Tis good, I apprehend it.—
  To kill one's self is meat that we must take
  Like pills, not chew'd, but quickly swallow it;
  The smart o' th' wound, or weakness of the hand,
  May else bring treble torments.

Flam. I have held it
   A wretched and most miserable life,
   Which is not able to die.

Vit. Oh, but frailty!
   Yet I am now resolv'd; farewell, affliction!
   Behold, Brachiano, I that while you liv'd
   Did make a flaming altar of my heart
   To sacrifice unto you, now am ready
   To sacrifice heart and all. Farewell, Zanche!

Zan. How, madam! do you think that I 'll outlive you;
   Especially when my best self, Flamineo,
   Goes the same voyage?

Flam. O most loved Moor!

Zan. Only, by all my love, let me entreat you,
   Since it is most necessary one of us
   Do violence on ourselves, let you or I
   Be her sad taster, teach her how to die.

Flam. Thou dost instruct me nobly; take these pistols,
   Because my hand is stain'd with blood already:
   Two of these you shall level at my breast,
   The other 'gainst your own, and so we 'll die
   Most equally contented: but first swear
   Not to outlive me.

Vit. and Zan. Most religiously.

Flam. Then here 's an end of me; farewell, daylight.
   And, O contemptible physic! that dost take
   So long a study, only to preserve
   So short a life, I take my leave of thee. [Showing the pistols.
   These are two cupping-glasses, that shall draw
   All my infected blood out. Are you ready?

Both. Ready.

Flam. Whither shall I go now? O Lucian, thy ridiculous purgatory! to
   find Alexander the Great cobbling shoes, Pompey tagging points, and
   Julius Cæsar making hair-buttons, Hannibal selling blacking, and
   Augustus crying garlic, Charlemagne selling lists by the dozen, and
   King Pepin crying apples in a cart drawn with one horse!

Whether I resolve to fire, earth, water, air,
Or all the elements by scruples, I know not,
Nor greatly care.—Shoot! shoot!
Of all deaths, the violent death is best;
For from ourselves it steals ourselves so fast,
The pain, once apprehended, is quite past.
                    [They shoot, and run to him, and tread upon him.

Vit. What, are you dropped?

Flam. I am mix'd with earth already: as you are noble,
  Perform your vows, and bravely follow me.

Vit. Whither? to hell?

Zan. To most assur'd damnation?

Vit. Oh, thou most cursed devil!

Zan. Thou art caught——

Vit. In thine own engine. I tread the fire out
  That would have been my ruin.

Flam. Will you be perjured? what a religious oath was Styx, that the gods never durst swear
by, and violate! Oh, that we had such an oath to minister, and to be so well kept in our courts
of justice!

Vit. Think whither thou art going.

Zan. And remember
  What villainies thou hast acted.

Vit. This thy death
  Shall make me, like a blazing ominous star,
  Look up and tremble.

Flam. Oh, I am caught with a spring!

Vit. You see the fox comes many times short home;
  'Tis here prov'd true.

Flam. Kill'd with a couple of braches!

Vit. No fitter offing for the infernal furies,
  Than one in whom they reign'd while he was living.

Flam. Oh, the way 's dark and horrid! I cannot see:
  Shall I have no company?

Vit. Oh, yes, thy sins
  Do run before thee to fetch fire from hell,
  To light thee thither.

Flam. Oh, I smell soot,
  Most stinking soot! the chimney 's afire:
  My liver 's parboil'd, like Scotch holly-bread;
  There 's a plumber laying pipes in my guts, it scalds.
  Wilt thou outlive me?

Zan. Yes, and drive a stake
  Through thy body; for we 'll give it out,
  Thou didst this violence upon thyself.

Flam. Oh, cunning devils! now I have tried your love,
  And doubled all your reaches: I am not wounded.
                              [Flamineo riseth.
  The pistols held no bullets; 'twas a plot
  To prove your kindness to me; and I live
  To punish your ingratitude. I knew,
  One time or other, you would find a way
  To give me a strong potion. O men,
  That lie upon your death-beds, and are haunted
  With howling wives! ne'er trust them; they 'll re-marry
  Ere the worm pierce your winding-sheet, ere the spider
  Make a thin curtain for your epitaphs.
  How cunning you were to discharge! do you practise at the Artillery
  yard? Trust a woman? never, never; Brachiano be my precedent. We lay
  our souls to pawn to the devil for a little pleasure, and a woman makes
  the bill of sale. That ever man should marry! For one Hypermnestra
  that saved her lord and husband, forty-nine of her sisters cut their
  husbands' throats all in one night. There was a shoal of virtuous
  horse leeches! Here are two other instruments.

Enter Lodovico, Gasparo, still disguised as Capuchins

Vit. Help, help!

Flam. What noise is that? ha! false keys i' th 'court!

Lodo. We have brought you a mask.

108

Flam. A matachin it seems by your drawn swords.
  Churchmen turned revelers!

Gas. Isabella! Isabella!

Lodo. Do you know us now?

Flam. Lodovico! and Gasparo!

Lodo. Yes; and that Moor the duke gave pension to
  Was the great Duke of Florence.

Vit. Oh, we are lost!

Flam. You shall not take justice forth from my hands,
  Oh, let me kill her!—I 'll cut my safety
  Through your coats of steel. Fate 's a spaniel,
  We cannot beat it from us. What remains now?
  Let all that do ill, take this precedent:
  Man may his fate foresee, but not prevent;
  And of all axioms this shall win the prize:
  'Tis better to be fortunate than wise.

Gas. Bind him to the pillar.

Vit. Oh, your gentle pity!
  I have seen a blackbird that would sooner fly
  To a man's bosom, than to stay the gripe
  Of the fierce sparrow-hawk.

Gas. Your hope deceives you.

Vit. If Florence be i' th' court, would he would kill me!

Gas. Fool! Princes give rewards with their own hands,
  But death or punishment by the hands of other.

Lodo. Sirrah, you once did strike me; I 'll strike you
  Unto the centre.

Flam. Thou 'lt do it like a hangman, a base hangman,
  Not like a noble fellow, for thou see'st
  I cannot strike again.

Lodo. Dost laugh?

Flam. Wouldst have me die, as I was born, in whining?

Gas. Recommend yourself to heaven.

Flam. No, I will carry mine own commendations thither.

Lodo. Oh, I could kill you forty times a day,
  And use 't four years together, 'twere too little!
  Naught grieves but that you are too few to feed
  The famine of our vengeance. What dost think on?

Flam. Nothing; of nothing: leave thy idle questions.
  I am i' th' way to study a long silence:
  To prate were idle. I remember nothing.
  There 's nothing of so infinite vexation
  As man's own thoughts.

Lodo. O thou glorious strumpet!
  Could I divide thy breath from this pure air
  When 't leaves thy body, I would suck it up,
  And breathe 't upon some dunghill.

Vit. You, my death's-man!
  Methinks thou dost not look horrid enough,
  Thou hast too good a face to be a hangman:
  If thou be, do thy office in right form;
  Fall down upon thy knees, and ask forgiveness.

Lodo. Oh, thou hast been a most prodigious comet!
  But I 'll cut off your train. Kill the Moor first.

Vit. You shall not kill her first; behold my breast:
  I will be waited on in death; my servant
  Shall never go before me.

Gas. Are you so brave?

Vit. Yes, I shall welcome death,
  As princes do some great ambassadors;
  I 'll meet thy weapon half-way.

Lodo. Thou dost tremble:
  Methinks, fear should dissolve thee into air.

Vit. Oh, thou art deceiv'd, I am too true a woman!
  Conceit can never kill me. I 'll tell thee what,

110

I will not in my death shed one base tear;
  Or if look pale, for want of blood, not fear.

Gas. Thou art my task, black fury.

Zan. I have blood
  As red as either of theirs: wilt drink some?
  'Tis good for the falling-sickness. I am proud:
  Death cannot alter my complexion,
  For I shall ne'er look pale.

Lodo. Strike, strike,
  With a joint motion. [They strike.

Vit. 'Twas a manly blow;
  The next thou giv'st, murder some sucking infant;
  And then thou wilt be famous.

Flam. Oh, what blade is 't?
  A Toledo, or an English fox?
  I ever thought a culter should distinguish
  The cause of my death, rather than a doctor.
  Search my wound deeper; tent it with the steel
  That made it.

Vit. Oh, my greatest sin lay in my blood!
  Now my blood pays for 't.

Flam. Th' art a noble sister!
  I love thee now; if woman do breed man,
  She ought to teach him manhood. Fare thee well.
  Know, many glorious women that are fam'd
  For masculine virtue, have been vicious,
  Only a happier silence did betide them:
  She hath no faults, who hath the art to hide them.

Vit. My soul, like to a ship in a black storm,
  Is driven, I know not whither.

Flam. Then cast anchor.
  Prosperity doth bewitch men, seeming clear;
  But seas do laugh, show white, when rocks are near.
  We cease to grieve, cease to be fortune's slaves,
  Nay, cease to die by dying. Art thou gone?
  And thou so near the bottom? false report,

111

Which says that women vie with the nine Muses,
For nine tough durable lives! I do not look
Who went before, nor who shall follow me;
No, at my self I will begin the end.
While we look up to heaven, we confound
Knowledge with knowledge. Oh, I am in a mist!

Vit. Oh, happy they that never saw the court,
  Nor ever knew great men but by report! [Vittoria dies.

Flam. I recover like a spent taper, for a flash,
  And instantly go out.
  Let all that belong to great men remember th' old wives' tradition, to
  be like the lions i' th' Tower on Candlemas-day; to mourn if the sun
  shine, for fear of the pitiful remainder of winter to come.
  'Tis well yet there 's some goodness in my death;
  My life was a black charnel. I have caught
  An everlasting cold; I have lost my voice
  Most irrecoverably. Farewell, glorious villains.
  This busy trade of life appears most vain,
  Since rest breeds rest, where all seek pain by pain.
  Let no harsh flattering bells resound my knell;
  Strike, thunder, and strike loud, to my farewell! [Dies.

Enter Ambassadors and Giovanni

Eng. Ambass. This way, this way! break open the doors! this way!

Lodo. Ha! are we betray'd?
  Why then let 's constantly all die together;
  And having finish'd this most noble deed,
  Defy the worst of fate, nor fear to bleed.

Eng. Ambass. Keep back the prince: shoot! shoot!

Lodo. Oh, I am wounded!
  I fear I shall be ta'en.

Giov. You bloody villains,
  By what authority have you committed
  This massacre?

Lodo. By thine.

Giov. Mine!

Lodo. Yes; thy uncle, which is a part of thee, enjoined us to 't:
  Thou know'st me, I am sure; I am Count Lodowick;
  And thy most noble uncle in disguise
  Was last night in thy court.

Giov. Ha!

Lodo. Yes, that Moor thy father chose his pensioner.

Giov. He turn'd murderer!
  Away with them to prison, and to torture:
  All that have hands in this shall taste our justice,
  As I hope heaven.

Lodo. I do glory yet,
  That I can call this act mine own. For my part,
  The rack, the gallows, and the torturing wheel,
  Shall be but sound sleeps to me: here 's my rest;
  I limn'd this night-piece, and it was my best.

Giov. Remove these bodies. See, my honour'd lord,
  What use you ought make of their punishment.
  Let guilty men remember, their black deeds
  Do lean on crutches made of slender reeds.

* * * *

Instead of an epilogue, only this of Martial supplies me:

Hæc fuerint nobis præmia, si placui.

For the action of the play, 'twas generally well, and I dare affirm, with the joint testimony of some of their own quality (for the true imitation of life, without striving to make nature a monster,) the best that ever became them: whereof as I make a general acknowledgment, so in particular I must remember the well-approved industry of my friend Master Perkins, and confess the worth of his action did crown both the beginning and end.

Made in the USA
Lexington, KY
30 December 2013